chasing
the
white witch

chasing
the
white witch

A NOVEL

marina cohen

DUNDURN
TORONTO

Editor: Shannon Whibbs
Design: Jennifer Scott
Printer: Webcom

Library and Archives Canada Cataloguing in Publication

Cohen, Marina
  Chasing the white witch / written by Marina Cohen.

Issued also in electronic formats.
ISBN 978-1-55488-964-8

  I. Title.

PS8605.O378C43 2011   jC813'.6   C2011-901873-X

1 ' 2   3   4   5   15   14   13   12   11

 Conseil des Arts du Canada Canada Council for the Arts Canada ONTARIO ARTS COUNCIL
CONSEIL DES ARTS DE L'ONTARIO

We acknowledge the support of the Canada Council for the Arts and the Ontario Arts Council for our publishing program. We also acknowledge the financial support of the Government of Canada through the Canada Book Fund and Livres Canada Books, and the Government of Ontario through the Ontario Book Publishing Tax Credit and the Ontario Media Development Corporation.

Care has been taken to trace the ownership of copyright material used in this book. The author and the publisher welcome any information enabling them to rectify any references or credits in subsequent editions.

J. Kirk Howard, President

Printed and bound in Canada.
www.dundurn.com

Dundurn
3 Church Street, Suite 500
Toronto, Ontario, Canada
M5E 1M2

Gazelle Book Services Limited
White Cross Mills
High Town, Lancaster, England
LA1 4XS

Dundurn
2250 Military Road
Tonawanda, NY
U.S.A. 14150

To my brother, Rob, and my cousin, Lisa,
who contributed to this novel without knowing it

Acknowledgements

I would like to send a heartfelt thank you to the following people: to readers, Dr. David Jenkinson, Natalie Hyde, Jaime Cohen, Jane Ross, and 6R; to my husband, Michael Cohen, for all his love and support; to the Ontario Arts Council for their generous support via the Writer's Reserve program; to all the amazing staff at Dundurn Press, including president and publisher, Kirk Howard, associate publisher and editorial director, Michael Carroll, publicist, Karen McMullin, and my wonderful editor, Shannon Whibbs.

1

This whole mess began when my fifteen-year-old brother, Jordan (who happens to be the biggest moron on the face of the earth), started bugging me about my first-ever zit. It didn't help that the thing was huge — okay, ginormous — and dead-centre on the tip of my nose. Even with a ton of concealer caked on my face, I felt like I should have been hauling a sleigh full of presents on a foggy winter's night instead of pushing a shopping cart through the Thanksgiving-weekend crowds at the Supersave.

"Head for cover! She's going to blow!" Jordan's voice echoed up the vegetable aisle, attracting scads of attention toward me and the glowing bump festering on my face. As if that wasn't bad enough, he then pretended to dive under the broccoli table, like my nose warranted some sort of code-red, lock-down measures. Honestly, after twelve-and-a-half years of teasing at the hands of my brother, a.k.a., El Doofus, you'd think I'd have grown a thicker skin.

"You're a funny guy, Jor," I said, forcing a smile. I narrowed my eyes and fixed them on the watermelon stand at the far end of the aisle. "You should consider a career as a comedian." I imagined a particularly deformed melon was Jordan's head. Then I pictured myself heaving it high in the air and sending it crashing onto the cold tile floor where it would explode into a wet pile of pinkish mush. A sliver of a grin tugged at my mouth.

"I can hear you," said Jordan, materializing in front of the shopping cart. He scanned the air with great exaggeration. "But I can't see you behind the mountain in front of your nose. Oh wait a minute — that *is* your nose! *Eehah, eehah, eehah.*" He laughed like a drunken mule.

Now, normally I tried my best not to let Jordan know he was getting to me, but from where I stood, the temptation was too great. My lip curled. I hunched my shoulders and dropped my chin. I tightened my grip on the shopping cart and was poised to plow him over like the insignificant dust-mite he was, when my mother emerged from behind, lugging a bag of yams. She stopped, sized up the situation, and rolled her eyes.

"Leave your sister alone, Jordan."

"Wha'd *I* do?" He did his best to look innocent.

She shook her head and let the yams plunk into the cart. They rolled off the frozen turkey that could feed an entire village, and squashed the box containing pumpkin pie. "I should have known better than to think you two would be any help to me whatsoever."

"I didn't do anything," Jordan protested. "It's not my fault Claire's growing a second head."

I glowered at him, but that amused him all the more. My mother offered me a look oozing with pity and sighed, at which point I could seriously feel the steam rising out of my skull.

"Stop pointing out Claire's blemish, Jordan. She's very sensitive about it." She smiled at me apologetically and then headed toward the checkout.

Blemish? Who uses that word anymore? Sometimes I swear my mother was born a century ago and got sucked through some sort of time warp. And *sensitive?* Well, I guess that's what they call it when you want to dig a hole in the desert and live in it until your face clears. Ten to twenty years should do it.

Ah well. *There's a pearl in many an oyster, if you're willing to dig through gelatinous gunk to find 'em —* as my dad always says. (My dad says a lot of strange things.) But I get it. My pearl was the fact that it was the Saturday afternoon of a long weekend. I had a whole two and a half days for my skin to clear — if it didn't, Jordan would be the least of my worries. His nasty comments would be like sticky-sweet compliments compared to what Hollis Van Horn would say. I shuddered at the thought.

Hollis was my sworn enemy. She was everything I wasn't. Thick, blond hair cascading down her back. Long, lean legs that ended at her chin. Sparkling blue eyes. A voice that could charm hornets. She was the most popular girl in the seventh grade, and for some reason, she never missed a chance to humiliate me.

Like the time in fifth grade when I came to school wearing two different shoes. Totally *not* my fault. My old beagle, Cyrus, has this annoying little habit — he stashes things. Mostly *my* things. All I could find that day was one white Nike and an old black pump. I was mortified, but what could I do? I wore extra-long jeans and walked really slowly. I'm sure I would have gotten away with it, except for Hollis, who noticed my shoe malfunction and blabbed it to the whole class.

And then in sixth grade, I accidentally plucked all my eyebrows trying to create that supermodel look. It started with a single hair here and there, you know, just to tidy things up, and next thing I knew, *whoosh*, they were gone. My bald forehead would have stayed safely hidden behind the new bangs I'd hastily given myself, were it not for Hollis's eagle-eyes and big, fat mouth. Even now, the thought of it makes my cheeks blister with anger — not to mention my eyebrows itch.

"Wanna tomato?" said Jordan, tossing a ripe one in my direction. "Oh, I see you already have one — stuck to your face!"

I'd released the shopping cart just in time to catch the innocent victim before it splatted at my feet. I sighed and returned the tomato to its stand.

Yes, as mind-boggling as it may seem, Jordan was nothing compared to Hollis. At least with Jordan you knew what you were up against. Hollis was subtler than a snake and meaner than a skillet full of scorpions. If I showed up Tuesday morning with the planet Mars orbiting the tip of my nose, Hollis and her friends would never let me live it down.

Jordan began humming "Rudolph the Red-Nosed Reindeer" as we approached the check-out. I was about to tell him that he was attracting hounds, when I heard her.

From somewhere behind me, a high-pitched trill of a voice twittered through the Supersave. Unmistakably Hollis.

My stomach bottomed out. I couldn't let her see my face like this. I danced on the spot like my feet were on fire, but there was nowhere to run — nowhere to hide. I wanted to shrivel up and die, or spontaneously combust. But since neither was an option, I did the only thing left for me to do.

ALIENS CURED MY ARTHRITIS announced the head-line in bold black letters. I snatched the latest copy of the tabloid magazine from the rack beside the checkout and just as I managed to bury my shame between the pages — it happened.

A tiny paperback book, no larger than a thank-you card, slipped from the metal rack overhead. It fluttered to the ground, landing open at my feet. For a second, the world around me dissolved. I stared in amazement at the words at the top of the page. Slowly, I bent down, lifted the book and examined the cover. Was it possible? The answer to my prayers? Right here, in my hot little hands? For once in my life, luck was on my side.

My mother was too busy organizing the food on the conveyor belt and Jordan was too engrossed in a sports magazine to notice when I slipped the little green book between the cans of cranberry sauce. Then, just as soon as the cashier scanned my little treasure, I snatched it back and jammed it into my pocket. I promised myself I'd sneak a five-dollar bill into Mom's wallet just as soon as we got home to make up for it.

So there I stood, grinning to myself like I'd just won the lottery. Hollis had miraculously passed by without seeing me and I was now in possession of a book that was going to fix my life. At least, that was the plan.

2

Remedies, Rituals, and Incantations.

I sat on the edge of my bed, running my index finger across the faded black print on the mossy green cover. There was no accompanying photo. No illustration. Not even a symbol. Nothing that might divulge any clue as to the book's contents. I flipped through the fifty-some miniature pages before returning to examine the cover again. I tilted the book slightly, catching the light. Shimmering in the deep, mossy green was a leafy pattern. My eyes wandered from the title to the author's name emblazoned across the bottom in fancy black script:

The White Witch

I'd seen loads of little books like this at the check-out in the past: *Cheeses and Chutneys, The Best of Bananas, Lose Inches from Your Ankles.* They were all the same — perfectly designed to attract impulsive shoppers with zero willpower. Was it worth the five bucks I slipped into Mom's wallet? Maybe. Then again, maybe not.

Cyrus, who had been lying on the floor at the end of my bed, raised his head, pointed his wrinkled, prune-like nose at me, and snorted.

I frowned. "Quit judging me, Cyrus." He snorted again (Cyrus always wants the last word), and laid his head back on his front paws to let me know he'd said his piece. I tossed the book aside and flopped backward, plunging into the feathery softness of my duvet. "You're right. I admit it. I've sunk to an all-time low."

"Lights out, Claire!" called my mother from the hallway.

"Five minutes!" I hollered back, in the most sincere voice I could manage.

"Make sure you get tons of beauty sleep — you need it! *Eehah, eehah, eehah ...*"

"Jordan! Leave your sister alone ..." My mother's voice faded into something more threatening, but I couldn't have cared less. Jordan could bungee-jump over cactuses using spaghetti as far as I was concerned.

New conviction coursed through my veins. I snatched the book from beside me, skipped past all the boring stuff — the foreword, the table of contents, the chapter introductions — and found the exact page I'd seen staring up at me in the grocery store. I read it out loud.

Acne Remedy
1 cup natural yogurt
3 tbsp. oatmeal
100 g Limburger cheese
6 cloves crushed garlic

In a small wooden bowl, using fingertips, mix all ingredients into a paste. Stand in front of a mirror and apply to face while chanting three times:

I feel the magic deep within me,
By the power and energy of three times three.
Blisters, boils, bubbles be gone,
Cleanse my pores, cleanse 'til dawn!

Let paste dry on face overnight. Wash thoroughly in the morning.

Underneath it was a remedy for diarrhea and on the next page, a really complex cure for ingrown toenails. But I spent little time examining those before returning my gaze to what I hoped was the magic miracle that would exile my evil pimple and clear the battleground to avoid any future uprisings.

I did a brief mental check. I was pretty sure we had all the ingredients — except maybe the Limburger. Dad *was* sort of a cheese-a-holic though, so if not Limburger, I figured he'd have a good substitute. But how to go about preparing my potion unnoticed? I decided it best to wait until everyone was asleep before raiding the refrigerator.

My parents were fairly predictable people. Mom usually went to bed sometime between ten and ten-thirty. She'd read a few pages of a big, fat romance novel with some muscular guy with long wavy hair on the cover until she'd drift off. Dad stayed up later to watch all his legal shows (he liked to think of himself as an investigator, district attorney, and forensic psychologist all rolled into one). At least once he headed up to bed he'd be out in a matter of minutes. Jordan, as usual, would be my biggest obstacle.

Jordan got to watch TV with dad. At eleven, he had to go to his room, but he always stayed up way past then playing games on his laptop or phone. I know because I'd heard him brag about it a zillion times to all his buddies. Yes, Jordan would be a problem. I'd have to make sure he was asleep before I began skulking around the house. If he caught me, he'd rat me out for sure — Jordan's middle name is Rat. El Doofus Rat Murphy. I'm thinking of buying him monogrammed towels for his birthday.

So there I lay, impatiently watching the glowing digital numbers on my clock change and change again. I must have nodded off at some point, because next thing I knew, it was midnight — the *Witching Hour*. How fitting.

I poked a toe at the floor, testing the ground tentatively. Once I was certain Cyrus wasn't lying there, I slipped out from under the covers and crept toward the door. I opened it a crack. Not even the tiniest sliver of light snaked out from under Jordan's closed door. Perfect.

I tiptoed across the landing and down the stairs. I couldn't risk switching on the lights so I groped around the kitchen in the shadows. My little green book was tucked neatly into the pocket of my pajamas. Luckily, I'd memorized the recipe.

Unfortunately, the only wooden bowl we had was the size of Arizona. I really wanted to follow the instructions as closely as possible, in case I got it wrong and managed to turn my face purple or grow a beard or something, so I retrieved the monster bowl from under the kitchen island and placed it on the counter.

Next — the yogurt and cheese. The fridge light went on automatically so I didn't have to dig blindly through long-forgotten leftovers or half-rotten fruit. I snatched a plastic yogurt tub and fished through the cold-cut compartment, locating a hunk of mouldy blue cheese. It wasn't Limburger, but hey, it was better than a kick in the shins with a frozen Ugg. I shut the door and the sudden shift from light to darkness sent a million glowing dots swarming in front of me. I staggered blindly toward the counter, stubbing my toes in the corner. A single yelp escaped my lips before I managed to stifle myself. I scrunched my toes, letting the pain dissolve, but it was too late. Cyrus's jingle-jangle tags and *click-click-clicking* of his nails across the ceramic tiles interrupted the silence.

Snorfle.

"I may not be able to see you, Cyrus," I hissed, "but don't think for a second I don't know that look in your eye. Now, could you please just be quiet and stay out of my way?" I heard Cyrus slide to the ground, grunting once more just to let me know who was boss.

I got a spoon from the cutlery drawer and a cup from the cabinet. I measured out the yogurt and let it splat into the wooden bowl, plopping the hunk of cheese into the middle of it. My mother kept all the cereal in large plastic containers. I found the oatmeal, grabbed a handful and tossed it into the mixture.

Then I paused. The final ingredient required a bit of thought. A trio of wire baskets hung in the corner of the kitchen. There were a few oranges and some bananas in the lower basket, kiwis in the middle one, and fresh garlic in the top basket.

I shook my head. Nuh-uh. The combination of knives and darkness was a recipe for bloodshed. I couldn't afford to lose a finger, so I opted for the fridge again where we kept a jar of pre-chopped garlic fermenting in oil. I snatched the jar and opened it. A cloud of hazy-stink assaulted my nostrils.

"Whew!" I said, fanning the air around me. I decided if this potion didn't work, I could always try rubbing one of my best friend Paula-Jean Fanelli's garlic-eggplant sandwiches on my face and hope for the best. For a second, I contemplated exactly what one clove of chopped garlic might look like, and then dumped in the whole jar just to be on the safe side.

Done.

I rubbed my hands together in anticipation and then dipped my fingers into the cool, mushy concoction. I mixed and mashed. I slid and swirled. The oatmeal was lumpy. The garlic was slippery. The cheese was stinky.

Minus the foul odour, I was almost starting to enjoy the experience when suddenly, the lights went on.

3

"What the heck are you doing?" demanded Jordan. He examined me with a look of carefully balanced amusement and suspicion. "And what is that disgusting smell?"

I froze. I was caught red-handed — or white-lumpy-handed, anyway. I could tell by the evil glint in Jordan's eye this wasn't going to end well. I had to think fast.

"I, er … I, um … midnight snack," I announced firmly.

Jordan's eyes narrowed. They volleyed from my face to the enormous bowl and back again. He wasn't buying it. I'd have to be more convincing. I raised my chin and one eyebrow (luckily I had eyebrows again), and without taking my eyes off him, I scooped up a handful of lumpy paste and pressed it into my mouth. "*Mmm*," I said, forcing myself to swallow. "Want some?" I held out the bowl to him.

Jordan blinked twice and shoved it away. "You're so weird, Claire." He reached down and gave Cyrus a scratch behind the ear. "Next time, try using a spoon, you slob." He turned and left the kitchen.

As soon as I heard the stairs groan under his weight, I snatched a dishtowel and wiped my hands. I tore open the fridge, grabbed a carton of orange juice, and gulped down its entire contents to try and get rid of the nasty taste. My stomach bubbled. Clearly, the orange juice was not making friends with the yogurt and cheese. I took a few long drawn breaths to let my insides settle. My tongue was burning from the garlic. I tried scrubbing it with the dish sponge, but that only made it worse.

Cyrus was staring at me the whole time. He had this irritating way of making me feel like a total idiot.

"What?" I demanded.

You belong in a yard sale, his amber eyes seemed to say.

I turned my back on him. What did he know about my problems? He was just a dumb old dog. It wasn't like *he* had to worry about other animals whispering about *him* behind his back if he got fleas or kennel-cough. I, on the other hand, had Little Miss Perfect and her gang of gossiping gargoyles to deal with. I was tired of all of them picking on me. Especially Hollis.

And as if her bullying wasn't bad enough, Hollis had this little giggle and this way of pursing her lips and tilting her head that everyone, including the teachers, found irresistible. She got away with tons of junk.

Just last week she'd managed to wriggle her way out of schoolyard cleanup by claiming she had a *slight migraine*. So while the rest of us seventh-grade suckers trudged through the mucky yard gathering disgusting old wrappers, slimy banana peels, pop cans, and other unidentifiable trash, she was probably lying in the office with an ice pack on her forehead, humming to herself, and thinking up new ways to destroy my life. Just the thought of it made my blood sizzle.

I gathered up my bowl, switched off the light, and side-stepped Cyrus, the judgmental beagle. I headed upstairs to the solitude of the bathroom to continue my magical remedy. By Monday morning, my pimple would be ancient history and Hollis and the rest of the girls would have to find some other target for their poisonous arrows.

"Don't bother following," I called over my shoulder.

Cyrus ignored me as usual, trotting up the stairs and right into the bathroom alongside me. I sighed and repeated my best I-know-you-can't-see-me-but-I'm-frowning-at-you-anyway scowl before poking my head out the door to make sure Jordan wasn't lurking nearby. Satisfied the coast was clear, I shut the door.

I switched on the lights and stood staring at myself in the mirror for the longest time. A thought began to swell in my mind. I pounced on it and tried to squelch it, but it slipped free and ran rampant through my brain: *Why can't I look more like Hollis Van Horn?* Those sea-foam eyes. That long hair with alternating honey and gold highlights. Those perfect teeth. That perfect smile. That perfect nose.

I sighed and opened a drawer. I took out a hair band and forced the mud-coloured frizz off my blotchy face. Digging into my pajama pocket, I withdrew the little white book and laid it open on the counter next to the sink. I took a deep breath and cleared my throat. "Here goes nothing," I said, scooping up a handful of the reeking remedy. I began smearing the paste all over my face, all the while chanting:

I feel the magic deep within me,
By the power and energy of three times three.
Blisters, boils, bubbles be gone,
Cleanse my pores, cleanse 'til dawn!

I began tentatively, pronouncing each syllable with great care until I'd completed the entire verse once. The second time, the words began to flow, picking up speed, filling the contours of my mouth before spilling from my lips. By the third time, the rhyme spewed out of me with absolute confidence, gushing forth from somewhere deep within, as if I were somehow born to speak it. As far as my face was concerned, I began to feel something. Was it magic? Was it power? Or was it just the weight of the cheese? I didn't care. Something told me this was going to work. I could feel it in my bones. I could smell the garlicky stench of victory in the air around me.

I looked down at Cyrus. He looked up at me. I blinked. He blinked. I waited for him to snorfle, or sneeze, or growl, but he didn't. I took it to be a good sign.

I grabbed a towel from the rack to cover my pillow — sleeping with this gloop on my face was going to be the real challenge. But I was up for it. I felt like I could march out of the bathroom and conquer the universe, even if I did look like a giant blancmange.

4

Sunlight crept through a crack in the blinds and tick-led my eyelashes. I yawned and stretched. My mind was soupy — oozing back and forth between dream and reality. I rolled out of bed and slogged toward the door.

It was Sunday morning. The turkey would be half-thawed and Mom would be frantically scouring and scrubbing the house for tomorrow's Thanksgiving feast. My best friend Paula-Jean, who I call Peej for short, would arrive in the afternoon for a sleepover. Mom said if I helped her clean, Paula-Jean and I could eat junk all day, do each other's makeup and nails, and stay up late watching *Clothes You Shouldn't Be Caught Dead In*. Mom even bought us a few teen trash mags to keep us occupied.

I had one foot into the hall when I suddenly remem-bered my face. My hands flew up just as Jordan came sauntering out of his room. Crusty flakes of dried yogurt and cheese flew everywhere as I desperately tried to hide my head.

Jordan stopped. He sized me up and down and shook his head. "I thought I told you to use a spoon." He swaggered down the stairs, calling over his shoulder, "And take a shower or something, Claire. You stink."

I stood there contemplating what was worse — the fact that Jordan had actually seen me like this, or the fact that he thought cheese and garlic crusted all over my face was somehow normal for me.

Oh well, I wasn't about to let Jordan ruin my morning. It was time to wash the guck off my face and bask in the glow of my clear complexion.

I raced into the bathroom and splashed warm water on my face, dissolving any remaining trace of cheesy oatmeal. I grabbed a towel, dried myself, and gazed into the mirror.

Huh? What was this? I couldn't believe my eyes. I rubbed them, but it was no illusion. How could this happen? How could this be? My pimple was not only still there, the wretched thing was bigger and redder than ever!

Half my body sunk into despair while the other half bristled with rage. The effect nearly knocked me off balance. I dropped to the floor cradling my head in my hands. Why didn't it work? Where did I go wrong? Are the healing properties of Limburger that much greater than those of blue cheese? Or was I just a failure at magic like I was at everything else?

I was about to lock myself in the bathroom for all eternity when I caught sight of the little green book lying casually next to the sink, exactly where I'd left it the night before. I wasted five bucks, a good night's sleep, and a hunk of Dad's precious blue cheese on the darn thing. I snatched the book from the counter and whipped it across the bathroom. It smacked against the wall and fluttered to the ground. I scrambled toward it. I was going to rip it — no, shred— no, flush it into oblivion, when I glimpsed the chapter introduction that I'd so recklessly skipped:

Remedies

Before any attempt to cure the physical being, one must be pure of mind and spirit. Therefore, take note of the following emotional ailments and cleanse thy character first:

Boils from anger,
Itch from greed,
Aches from envy,
Chills from ill deed,
Cuts from laziness,
Pains from pride,
Bloating from gluttony,
Wrinkles from snide,
Disease from resentment,
Dandruff from scorn,
Odour from neglect,
Fever from oaths unsworn.

What was this? *Cleanse thy character?* What the heck was that supposed to mean? Was this why my potion had flopped? I was supposed to *cleanse my character* first? Who knew? And how does one go about cleansing one's character, anyway? Soap? Detergent? Surely something biodegradable and ammonia-free. I read the words over and over. By about the tenth time, a spark of comprehension flashed in my brain.

Boils from anger. I supposed, in the grand scheme of life, a pimple could be considered a type of boil. And I had to admit, I was pretty much bursting with anger these past few days. I was annoyed at Jordan. I was fuming at Hollis. I was even irritated with poor Cyrus. I had to face the facts: I was one irate individual.

Okay. So first I had to cleanse my character. I got it. Trouble was, I flipped through page after page, but the stupid book offered no instructions as to how to rid oneself of anger. All I could find was the puzzling poem, which ironically, had the effect of making me even angrier.

I went back to my bedroom, threw on a pair of jeans and a sweatshirt, shoved the book into my pocket, and stomped downstairs. I plunked myself into a chair in the kitchen and sat, arms crossed, glaring at the wall.

"Morning, Smiley," said my dad, strolling into the kitchen.

I glanced at him, grunted, and returned my gaze to a tiny brown fleck on the wall that may or may not have been the remnants of a bran flake I sneezed out last week.

My dad sighed. He pulled up a chair and put a hand on my arm. "Claire-bear, if you scrunched up your face any tighter it would disappear into itself." He smiled at me — the kind of smile that lets you know you're loved even if you are destined for a yard sale. And though I was clenching it pretty tightly, I could feel some of my anger slip away.

"Dad?" I asked. "How does a person get un-angry?"

"Un-angry, eh? Depends. Who or what are you mad at?"

"I dunno," I said. "Pretty much everyone and everything."

My father leaned back in his chair. He tilted his head as if he were thinking really hard. He scratched the dark stubble that had grown on his chin and cheeks overnight. I knew what was coming. I braced myself.

"I'm not sure how you get rid of anger," he said finally. "I guess you could try meditation. Or aromatherapy …"

Was it just my imagination, or was Dad leaning slightly away from me? I sniffed the air and decided that anger wasn't the only thing clinging desperately to my person.

"All I know for sure is," he continued, "*If you kick a stone, you'll hurt your foot.*"

And there it was. He'd lulled me into a false sense of security and then *wham!* hit me with one of his impossible sayings.

I stared at him through hooded eyes. "Thanks, Dad. Makes sense. Can't possibly see how that relates to my situation, though."

Dad smiled again. He stood up and patted me on the back. "I have faith in you, Claire. You're a pretty smart girl. You'll figure it out."

5

"Neon green is so you," I said holding Paula-Jean's index finger steady and letting the polish glide over her chipped nail.

"You think?" she said, holding her hand up and letting it catch the light. She tucked an unruly curl behind her ear with the opposite hand. "Because I don't feel like a very neon-greeny kind of person."

I frowned and yanked her hand back down onto my bed. "That's your problem, Peej. I know you better than you know yourself. You are definitely neon green. Exactly like Star Morningstar." I pointed to a picture in one of the magazines of a pop singer with long purple hair and neon-green lipstick and nails. "Trust me."

Whether she trusted me or not was debatable, but Paula-Jean did know me pretty well. She most likely figured I'd get my way in the end, so she surrendered her hand and let me paint away.

Before Paula-Jean arrived, I'd spent an hour helping Mom clean the house, an hour meditating in my room, an hour soaking in the tub using Mom's eucalyptus and lavender bath oil, and an hour watching the comedy channel. All the while, I mulled over Dad's weird saying until I was pretty sure I had it figured out: anger hurts no one except the person who's angry. With that in mind, I tried really hard to cleanse myself of all my frustrations. I was definitely no longer what you'd call *infuriated* or *irate*, but I admit I was still a bit grumpy. Then Paula-Jean came and that too changed.

Paula-Jean always had this way of making me feel like I didn't have a care in the world. She listened to all my troubles — really listened. And she wasn't the least bit judgmental. She told the funniest stories and always made me laugh. She was the best friend anyone could hope for. I hadn't told her about my magical midnight adventure yet, but I was working my way up to it.

As we sat there chatting about everything and nothing, I could feel my remaining worries and frustrations melt away. I even gave Jordan a friendly wave when he passed by in the hall and Cyrus, who was lying next to my bed, a loving pat on the head — being careful, of course, not to mess up my nails. I took a deep breath and exhaled slowly. The smell of garlic was history and for the first time in a long while I was at peace with the world.

"So, what do you think I should do about this zit?" I asked, as we lay at opposite ends of my bed, fanning our nails. "If I don't get rid of it before Monday, Hollis and the others will terrorize me for sure."

Paula-Jean looked right at me. She squinted. "What zit?"

I tilted my head and rolled my eyes. It wasn't like Paula-Jean to make light of something this serious.

"Very funny, Peej," I said pointing to the tip of my nose. "This zit. The one competing with Mount Everest."

Paula-Jean leaned forward and wrinkled her nose. She examined me thoroughly before shaking her head. "I don't see anything, Claire."

My spine straightened. Something was off. Paula-Jean was nothing if not honest. My hand flew up to my face in reflex. I touched my nose with my fingertip. There was no bump. No swelling. Nothing. *Nada*. My stomach somersaulted. *Could it possibly be?*

I sprang from my bed, hurdling Cyrus, and raced to my dresser. I looked in the mirror and nearly fell backward. My pimple had disappeared! Not just shrinking. Not just beginning to fade. But gone! Completely, totally, unmistakably *gone*!

Thoughts flipped around my brain like they were auditioning for Cirque du Soleil. Had the remedy really worked? Had I rid myself from enough anger? Had I cleansed my character enough to allow the garlic and cheese to take full effect? At some point between meditation and aromatherapy before Paula-Jean's arrival, my pimple had vanished. There was no other reasonable conclusion. It was magic, plain and simple.

I dug out the little green book from the pocket of my jeans and held it gingerly in my trembling hands. The fine hairs on the back of my neck stood on end. Although part of me had really wanted to believe the book had magical powers, the other part of me thought it was just a cheap ploy to rip off desperate fools such as myself. I gazed up at the flawless complexion staring back at me in the mirror and then back down at the book. My mouth went chalk-dry. My knees wobbled.

This book was real. It was magic. And it was all mine.

"What are you doing?" asked Paula-Jean. "What's that in your hand?"

For a second I'd forgotten all about her. How would I explain everything to Paula-Jean? Would she believe me? Or would she think I'd completely lost it? I decided there was only one way to find out. I took a deep breath and explained.

Paula-Jean sat silently listening to the whole story. Her big, brown eyes grew into saucers when I told her that my golf-ball-sized pimple had up and disappeared leaving no evidence of its existence and all because I'd glooped some home-made concoction onto my face, chanted a few simple words, and managed to get rid of my anger.

"Like magic ..." she sighed.

I nodded. "Like magic ..."

She stared down at the book, as if she wanted to touch it, but was somehow afraid. I stared down at it, too, finding myself curious as to what else my little treasure was capable of. I looked up at her just as a sliver of a grin snaked across my lips. She drew back and shook her head.

"No," she said waving her hands in front of her face. "Nuh-uh. I'm not getting involved in any weird magic stuff, Claire."

"Come on, Peej," I said. "Just one teensy-weensy spell."

"No way," she insisted. "If that book is really magic, you have no idea what you could be getting yourself into. What if something went wrong? What then?"

I dangled the book at her like it was some sort of giant hairy spider. She squeaked and dove for cover under my duvet.

"Don't be such a chicken, Peej," I scoffed. Then I let the book fall open to a random page. I lifted it up and let the words hover in front of me. "What could possibly go wrong?"

6

Avenging Curse

On the night of a New Moon, harvest a
branch from a yearling tree. By the flickering
glow of candlelight, thump the stick against
a thick rug while imagining the person who
has wronged you. Chant three times:

Injustice has been done unto me
I summon the power of three times three
Aches and pains, soreness and stitch,
Wake up in the morning with twinge and itch.

Compost branch to complete spell.

Paula-Jean looked at me like I had three heads. "You
can't possibly be serious."

"Why not?" I said. "It's not like he doesn't deserve it."

Paula-Jean shook her head. "You know, Claire,
sometimes I think I know you — totally get you — and
other times it's like you're this alien speaking some
freak language."

"It's just one teeny-tiny curse. Where's the harm in that? Besides," I shrugged, "it's not like he hasn't cursed me a thousand times."

"You see, Claire. Now, there's where you scare me. You don't see the difference between Jordan bugging you like any other big brother on the face of the earth — and you sneaking out in the middle of the night, maiming some poor, defenceless shrub, burning candles, and chanting weird voodoo stuff?"

"It's not voodoo, Peej — there's no doll involved. But now that you mention it …" I began flipping enthusiastically through the pages, but Paula-Jean snatched the book from my hands and slammed it shut.

She sighed and then switched strategies. "Look, didn't you skip some chapter introduction or something and miss some really important information? Shouldn't you at least read that first?"

I knew she was just trying to talk me out of my plan, but she did have a point. I wouldn't make the same mistake twice. I frowned and held out my hand. She reluctantly returned the book. I located the chapter introduction and read it out loud:

Incantations
Before preparing to cast out spells,
Listen closely, hark ye well:
Be wary of the three R rule you should:
Respect thyself, respect others, be respon-
    sible and good.
Seek no power from the suffering of others.

Treat all you meet as sisters and brothers.
For what goes out, returns threefold.
Ye have been warned, ye have been told.

"Warned!" shouted Paula-Jean, grabbing me by the shoulders and shaking me side to side violently. "Warned, Claire!"

"Yeah, yeah, yeah," I grumbled, wriggling out of her grasp and standing up. "Peej, everything has warnings these days. They don't mean anything. They're just legal mumbo-jumbo so you can't end up suing the company."

She rolled her eyes and sighed. "There you go scaring me again …"

"Let's just go through this logically, okay? First, I'm not seeking any *power* from Jordan's suffering, just a little enjoyment, right? And second, I am *totally* treating him like a brother — a *mean* brother …"

She narrowed her eyes and chewed her bottom lip. Then she pointed an accusing neon-green fingernail at me. "But what about the '*what goes out returns threefold*' part? What about that part, *genius?*" She flashed me a satisfied grin.

I thought about it for a second. I wasn't quite sure what to make of that line, but whatever it meant, I decided that if I could get back at Jordan for all his years of torment, it was definitely worth the risk. "Only one way to find out."

The rest of the day oozed along like a drowsy slug. My mom was now anxiously organizing the good cutlery, dishes, and fine crystal. Seriously — you'd think the queen was popping over tomorrow for dinner instead of my grandparents. Anyway, Mom enlisted Paula-Jean and me to help peel potatoes and yams while she ran out for some last-minute ingredients.

The whole time Mom was gone, Paula-Jean kept trying different tactics to talk me out of what she claimed was sheer madness. But she was wasting her time. I had my mind made up and I'd inherited my grandmother's stubborn gene. Besides, I just had to try the book out again. After all, there was still a slight possibility that my pimple had healed itself all on its own. Was it really magic? I needed to know.

According to the calendar, the New Moon began tonight. Even nature was on my side. And then, when Jordan walked into the kitchen, grabbed a pop from the fridge, yelled, "Hey, check this out!" and proceeded to pull his T-shirt over his head and drink the entire can through his shirt, letting out a huge belch, completely embarrassing me in front of my best friend, not to mention grossing her out, I knew there was no turning back.

We spent the rest of the day and the early evening, munching on junk food, watching reality shows on TV, and reading through the teen trash magazines Mom had bought for us. After we got ready for bed, I set my alarm for 11:30. I wasn't going to take any chances. If I fell asleep, I'd have to wait an entire month until the next New Moon. Paula-Jean wouldn't let up. She kept trying to convince me to drop the whole thing, right up until she conked out. Too excited to sleep, I just lay there listening to her snore until the alarm finally went off. The loud noise startled her, but I grabbed her mouth before she could scream and then flicked on the bedside lamp.

Paula-Jean sat up. "You are seriously going through with this?" she asked, staring at me with a sort of bleak resignation pooling in her eyes.

"Yup."

"And there's nothing I can say to talk you out of it?"

"Nope."

Paula-Jean huffed loudly. She stood up and pulled her jeans and a sweatshirt on over her pyjamas. "Okay, then. Let's do it."

You couldn't have pried the smile off my face with a crowbar as I grabbed my clothes and yanked them over my pajamas. I fished through my nightstand, located a flashlight, and with Paula-Jean close behind me, I crept to the door. The hallway was pitch-black. I pulled Paula-Jean out of my room and together we tiptoed down the stairs, slipped into our shoes, and stepped out the front door before Cyrus's little legs could catch up with us.

The autumn air was damp and cold. White smoke snaked from my nostrils, floated in the air for a moment, and then was snatched off by a bitter wind. Impatient winter seemed to be giving lazy fall a good hard shove and I suddenly found myself wishing I'd worn my jacket. I hugged my arms to my chest as I contemplated the best place to find a year-old tree.

"What are we waiting for? I'm freezing!" said Paula-Jean. "Just grab a branch already and let's go back inside."

I searched up the street and back down looking for my victim. It was dark out — darker than usual. Even with the streetlamps lit on one side, without the silver glow of the moon, the night sky seemed murky and somehow ominous. I clicked on the flashlight and a white beam sliced through the shadows. I would have been slightly nervous were it not for Paula-Jean hugging my right side.

"Come on, Claire," she huffed. "This isn't rocket science — just snap off a branch and let's go!"

"I can't just grab any old branch, Peej," I said, shining the light in her face. "The book said it had to be a yearling. You've got to follow the instructions perfectly, you know."

"Oh. 'Scuse me," she mumbled, slapping the flashlight away. "I forgot you were some kind of creepy magic expert."

I ignored her last comment and started walking toward the sidewalk. She ran to catch up and glued herself to me. Paula-Jean's thick mop of dark curls blew every which way as we headed down the street. She started to whine again, but I shot her a look that said, *I know what I'm doing*, to spare myself from any further arguments. I was on a mission — a deliciously daring and diabolical mission and I'd be lying if I said I wasn't enjoying every minute of it.

"Here we are," I said, standing in front of Mrs. Walker's house. I pressed the flashlight into Paula-Jean's hands and fixed the shaft of light on a particular plant with narrow scarlet leaves and magnificent late-harvest pink-and-orange fruit dangling from its limbs.

"Old Lady Walker? Have you completely lost it?" Paula-Jean stepped backward until she was almost standing in the middle of the road. She shone the flashlight on me like a spotlight. "She'll skin you alive with her trowel if you touched even a blade of her prefect grass!"

Paula-Jean was right. My courage sprung a leak. I felt it draining from me like water from a sieve. But I wasn't about to let her know I was getting nervous. I forced steadiness into my voice.

"First off, I'm not after Mrs. Walker's grass, am I? Second, how do you think she's going to find out? Do you think she has security cameras guarding the place?" I rolled my eyes for dramatic effect, but secretly I was scanning the house's dark brick exterior, looking for anything remotely resembling a lens.

Mrs. Walker lived and breathed for her meticulously manicured lawn and garden. You'd see her out in all kinds of weather trimming and pruning and planting and mulching. She'd shriek like a banshee at anyone who happened to wander off the sidewalk and take a single step on her perfectly edged lawn. If she caught me ripping a branch off her shrub — her brand-new shrub, no less — there was no telling what she'd do to me.

Trouble was, I didn't see any way around it. I knew Mrs. Walker had planted a dwarf winterberry euonymus a few months ago. The only reason I knew what a dwarf winterberry euonymus was is because Mrs. Walker insisted on telling me and my mother every painfully boring detail about the darn thing when we ran into her in the grocery store last week. I didn't know much of anything about shrubs — let alone dwarf winterberry euonymuses — but I guessed that since the bush was recently planted it couldn't be more than a year old.

"You stay here, Peej," I said, swallowing a baseball-sized lump that had formed at the back of my throat. "I'm going in."

Paula-Jean gave me a mock salute and wished me luck. I turned and slunk up the driveway, eyeing the unsuspecting shrub nestled snugly against the side of the porch. I was going to be quick — greased lightning — I told myself, as I crept toward the cluster of reddish-brown leaves. I grabbed hold of a nice thin little branch and was about to snap it off, when suddenly the front door flew open.

"Who's out there?" screeched Mrs. Walker. "Show yourself, you coward!"

No way was I leaving without my prize. Adrenaline surged through my veins as I yanked wildly at the branch. Pink fruit and scarlet leaves flew every which way and when the branch finally snapped, I fell backward into the junipers. The spiky foliage poked through my clothes and stabbed my skin.

"Stop! Tree vandal! I'll have your head!" Mrs. Walker screamed. Luckily she wasn't wearing her glasses. She couldn't see a thing without them.

I scrambled to my feet, and, holding the branch like the Olympic torch, I flew across the lawn toward Paula-Jean, who was already tearing up the pavement making a beeline for my house. I could hear Mrs. Walker hollering behind me, but from her mad ravings I could tell she hadn't recognized me. As I ran, the leaves and fruit of the dwarf winterberry euonymus blew off the branch one by one, scattering evidence of my tree massacre to the wind.

I caught up with Paula-Jean. We ran neck and neck until we reached my house and then slipped back inside the front door. I stood in the safety of my dark hallway panting and puffing, holding my branch like I'd captured an enemy flag.

Paula-Jean growled something unrecognizable and began slapping my shoulders. Her hand froze mid-air when the old clock in the living room chimed midnight.

7

The candle flickered, casting demon shadows on my bedroom wall. Paula-Jean sat silent and still — a little off to my left side, like she was worried the spell might go haywire and ricochet off the walls and onto her by accident. Cyrus was lying in his usual spot at my bedside. He raised his little eyebrows and then buried his snout deeper between his front paws as though he was avoiding certain disaster. The air was thick with anticipation, while the faint aroma of dwarf winterberry euonymus whispered into my nostrils.

I gripped the branch tightly in my right hand and then closed my eyes. I did my best to picture Jordan's goofy grin. I thought of all the millions of mean and nasty comments he'd made over the years. I thought about the time when I was seven and he got gum stuck in my hair. My parents had to practically shave me bald to get it all out. And the time he knocked me into a sea of mud — on photo day. I was a mess and although they let me do a retake for my personal portrait, there was nothing I could do about the class picture. And then there was the time he told Mom and Dad that *I* broke the chandelier when *he* was the one who dared me to throw a perfect spiral with his foam football. I had to pay for the chandelier with a whole five-months' worth of my allowance.

I struck the carpet with my branch once and became suddenly aware my lips had been moving independently of my brain. My little green book lay open in my lap, but I hadn't even glanced at it; I had blurted out the entire curse without even realizing it. The second time I made a conscious effort. I pronounced each word deliberately, thumping the stick three or four times, feeling all my anger and frustration toward Jordan sliding from my brain, down into my arm, through my hand, onto the stick ,and into the thick, beige carpet. The third time, it was like I was in some kind of weird trance. I thumped and thrashed and thwacked. I whipped and whomped and whacked. I beat that carpet so wildly the stick slipped from my hand, flew straight up in the air, and came down, smacking me right between the eyes, snapping me out of my stupor.

"Eeoowww!" I shouted, rubbing my forehead and turning toward Paula-Jean. "Did you see that? That branch attacked me!"

Paula-Jean stifled a giggle. "Serves you right, Claire. You were totally out of control."

Before I could stop him, Cyrus hoisted himself to his feet. He scrambled toward the stick and snatched it in his gooey jaws. He nudged the door open, and made off into the hall and down the stairs with the dwarf winterberry euonymus. I would have chased after him, but my body suddenly felt like a sack of dirty laundry. I fell backward into the carpet and sighed deeply. Lack of sleep had definitely caught up with me.

"So?" asked Paula-Jean, yawning. "Do you think it worked?" She wriggled into her sleeping bag and fluffed her pillow.

"No idea," I said. I barely had the energy to blow out the candle and crawl into my own sleeping bag. I lay there for a few moments thinking about Jordan and what I may or may not have done to him. A slight twinge of guilt flitted through my brain, but it was nothing that a deep yawn couldn't cure. "I guess we'll find out in the morning."

In a matter of minutes, Paula-Jean was snoring away. Although my body felt as though I'd just run three consecutive marathons, I couldn't manage to fall asleep. I twisted and turned. My back was itchy where the juniper needles had stabbed me. My forehead was sore where the branch had struck me. And for some reason, no matter what position I tried, I just couldn't get comfortable.

Morning light dribbled through the cracks in the blinds, snuffing out any remaining chance I had of getting a decent night's sleep. Paula-Jean yawned and stretched, turning toward me all bright-eyed and bushy-tailed.

She smiled. "Hey."

"Mm," I grunted. As I wriggled out of my sleeping bag, a dull ache rippled through my whole body. I groaned.

"What's wrong?" she asked.

"Nothing." I decided not to tell Paula-Jean I felt like I'd been in a train wreck. I just knew she'd find a way to connect my aches and pains to the *what goes out, returns threefold* and I was in no mood for any I-told-you-sos.

I got up and got dressed as quickly as my sore limbs would allow. Despite my fragile condition, I was anxious to see if my curse had actually had any effect on Jordan.

Paula-Jean and I sat at the breakfast table suspiciously still, our cereal getting soggier by the moment, eyeing each other and waiting for Jordan to arrive. When I heard his bedroom door creak open and his lumbering steps descending the stairs, my back straightened and my pulse quickened.

"This is it," I whispered. "This will tell us for sure if that book is magic."

Paula-Jean nodded once and then fixed her eyes on the doorway.

Jordan entered the kitchen rubbing his neck. He stopped short when he saw us sitting there like a couple of statues, gawking at him.

"You two freaks practising for the staring Olympics?"

I fumbled for my spoon and shovelled a heap of mushy cereal into my mouth and pretended to chew. All the while, I studied Jordan as he walked over to the fridge, opened it, got out the milk, and poured himself a tall glass. He kept moving his head side to side, bending his neck and rolling his shoulders. He reached around and rubbed the small of his back with one hand and then scratched his scalp.

My jaw dropped and mushy cereal leaked out of my mouth. I glanced at Paula-Jean who had the same stunned look on her face. But a sore neck was one thing: I needed to hear him say it. I needed confirmation. I clamped my mouth shut, swallowed the cereal, and dragged a sleeve across my face. "Ask him," I mouthed.

Paula-Jean shook her head violently.

"Ask him," I repeated, this time in a whisper.

She shook her head again, so I kicked her lightly under the table.

"You ask him. He's your brother," hissed Paula-Jean.

Jordan swung round to face us. He frowned. "Ask me what?" He was now rubbing his neck with his free hand, holding his milk with the other.

I cleared my throat. "Um ... well ... Paula-Jean was wondering ..." She shot me a fierce scowl. "... if you, er ... feel okay ..." I winced. Even *I* thought I sounded ridiculous.

Jordan narrowed his eyes. For a second I thought he was going to just ignore me, but then he set his glass down on the counter, folded his arms and said, "If you really wanna know, I feel horrible. Like I slept on a bed of nails."

8

"You gotta get rid of that thing," said Paula-Jean. She sat on the edge of my bed and pointed a trembling finger at my precious little green book. "I'm telling you, Claire, there's something wrong here. Very wrong."

"*Wrong?*" I shouted. My voice rose an entire octave. "What's *wrong* with a little magic? What's *wrong* with a little power?"

I turned the book over in my hands. It was the answer to my prayers. A magic book that could cure zits. That could put Jordan (and anyone else who crossed me) in their place. And that was only the beginning. The tip of the iceberg. Who knew what the book was really capable of? I flipped through the pages. Rheumatism Remedy. Rain-Making Ritual. *Luuuuvvvv Potionnnn ...* No way was I getting rid of this treasure. Not a chance. I hugged it close to my chest and stared at her defiantly.

Paula-Jean didn't say anything for the longest time. When she finally spoke, her voice was cautious. "Look, Claire ... it's like Mrs. Martin said in Social Studies the other day. Too much power in any one person's hands can be ... well ... *dangerous* ..." She had been staring at the carpet and when she looked up and our eyes met, I swear I saw a hint of fear flickering there.

That really set me off. She was supposed to be my best friend, after all — my caring, non-judgmental, best friend — so where did she get off sounding all high-and-mighty, looking at me like I was some kind of maniacal monster? Besides, my father had the monopoly on cryptic sayings.

"I don't believe you! How can you say such a rotten thing?" I yelled. "How could you think I'd do anything really terrible? All I did was cure my zit …"

"And thrash Jordan …"

"*Indirectly* thrash Jordan," I corrected her. "I never actually laid a finger on him. And why shouldn't I get back at him? Do I need to remind you that I'm the victim here?"

She looked me up and down with her big brown eyes and suddenly I didn't feel like much of a victim. That made me all the more angry. I stood up and turned my back on her. I walked to the window and pretended to look out at the empty yard, the bleak sky, and the bare branches. All the while I kept thinking that Paula-Jean should be happy for me. That she should be supportive. That she should be standing by my side, rejoicing in my new-found magical abilities. We were a team. Like Batman and Robin. Like Holmes and Watson. Like peanut butter and banana.

"You think I'm a horrible person, don't you?" I mumbled.

It was less of a question and more of an opportunity for her to redeem herself. I wanted her to say, *Oh no, Claire, you are the sweetest, most kind and generous person in the whole world.*

But she didn't.

"It's not that," she began. "It's just that … you're … well … you're impulsive, and …"

"*Impulsive? Who? Moi?*" I practically leapt over my bed and thrust the book in her face. "This book came to me for a reason," I said smugly. "I didn't find it. *It* found *me*." I narrowed my eyes. "I suppose you'd rather see it in someone else's hands? Someone like Hollis Van Horn?"

"I didn't say that," she countered.

"Aha!" I yelled. "But you were thinking it!"

Paula-Jean rolled her eyes. "Don't be ridiculous."

"Oh, so now I'm not only impulsive, I'm ridiculous, too!"

She sighed. "Enough, Claire. I'm not gonna sit here and argue with you. Keep your stupid book if you want. But don't come crying to me when something goes wrong."

Paula-Jean picked up her sleeping bag. She stood staring at me for a moment, waiting for me to stop her. But I didn't say a word. I just stood there scowling. She shook her head and began gathering up the rest of her things. I didn't move a muscle to help her. I just watched as she headed down the stairs, stepped into her shoes, got her jacket, and quietly closed the door behind her.

I spent the rest of the day sulking in my bedroom and hoping Paula-Jean would call to apologize, but she didn't. I came downstairs to say hello to my grandparents and my Uncle Rob and Aunt Theresa who had arrived for Thanksgiving dinner — but only because my mother forced me to.

My body ached all over. Even my taste buds were sore. When it was finally time to sit down to Mom's magnificent turkey dinner with all the trimmings, I wasn't even hungry. I just sat there staring at my plate, while Mom, Dad, Grandma Bea, Grandpa Joe, Uncle Rob, Aunt Theresa, Jordan (who looked like he'd gotten over his *twinge and itch* pretty quickly), and even Cyrus enjoyed the delicious food and good company.

By early evening, I was as miserable and achy as ever. Cyrus had hidden the dwarf winterberry euonymus branch somewhere and I couldn't find it. I needed to compost it to complete the spell, which I was sure was why I was still aching. And then, to top it all off, that night, when I went up to brush my teeth and get ready for bed, I was devastated to discover that my face was plagued with *four* new pimples!

I closed my eyes and took a deep cleansing breath. Lucky for me (and no thanks to Paula-Jean), I was still in possession of my little green book and there was plenty of garlic in the wire basket and loads of cheese in the fridge.

9

It was Tuesday morning — time to head back to school. The sky was a woolly grey mantle leaking cold drizzle into the morning air. I pulled my jacket hood over my head and dropped my chin to shield my face from the damp, chilly breeze. When I looked up, I saw Paula-Jean standing at our usual spot on the street corner. If she hadn't already been there, waiting for me, I'd have continued on my way alone.

We walked to school side by side, barely saying two words to each other. As we passed Mrs. Walker's house, Paula-Jean cast a sidelong glance my way. Though I kept my focus on the sleek cement, out of the corner of my eye, I could see a very lopsided dwarf winterberry euonymus and battered pink fruit strewn about the front lawn. I knew what Paula-Jean was thinking, but no way was I going to open my mouth and give her another opportunity to assault my good character.

At school, Paula-Jean and I hung sullenly around our lockers, waiting for the bell to ring. Suddenly, a nearby door swung open, almost smacking me square in the face.

Hollis Van Horn flounced into the hallway and breezed past Paula-Jean and I without so much as a ceremonial glance. It was like we were totally invisible. She

marina cohen

got about three steps past us when she stopped mid-stride. She sniffed the air and then turned and glared at me. She didn't say a single word — she didn't have to. I could feel the weight of her disapproval.

Beside me, Paula-Jean shifted side to side nervously. I couldn't believe her. If she were any kind of friend whatsoever, she'd have had the decency to tell me I was olfactorily offensive — that I reeked of garlic and cheese. I was going to say something to her, but I caught myself, remembering that we weren't speaking. All I could do was glare defiantly at Hollis and then watch helplessly as she wrinkled her perfect little nose. She swung round and ran up to her group of gangly gargoyles who almost immediately burst into laughter.

In class, I took my seat near Mrs. Martin's desk. I got out the writing assignment I'd managed to hastily complete Saturday morning before I'd gone to the Supersave with my mom and Jordan. I smoothed out the paper that had gotten a tad wrinkled under the weight of my lunch bag. I was always forgetting to fold things neatly like Mrs. Martin suggested and tuck them into my agenda or binder so they wouldn't crease. Luckily, new progressive rules dictated that teachers weren't allowed to deduct marks for wrinkles anymore.

Just as Mrs. Martin was about to collect our essays, Hollis fluttered across the floor and began whispering to her. My proximity to the teacher's desk allowed for maximum eavesdroppage.

"Um, Mrs. Martin," said Hollis, "I couldn't get my essay done because I'm in the Miss Teen Turnip Pageant next weekend at the Boxgrove County Fair and on Friday I discovered that my lucky pageant shoes had a horrible scuff. My mother insisted we spend the entire weekend searching for a new pair." She dangled a pretty pink slip of paper (that I'm absolutely certain was scented — yuk!) between her long, French-manicured claws. A note. No teacher could go against *the note*.

"No problem, Hollis," said Mrs. Martin, smiling warmly. "Just hand it in tomorrow."

I thought I was going to heave on the spot.

But I didn't.

"Ahem," I said.

Mrs. Martin and Hollis turned toward me at the same time.

I cleared my throat a second time and raised my eyebrows.

"Is there something you want to say, Claire?" asked Mrs. Martin.

I suppose the funny thing about Hollis and me was, though I could count a hundred reasons why I disliked her (graceful, gorgeous, popular being the top three), I could never figure out what I'd ever done to make her dislike me so much. I never did a thing to her. Not a single, solitary thing.

"Um, well, Mrs. Martin," I began. "Didn't you say on Friday that anyone who didn't complete their home-work wouldn't be allowed to take part in Fall Fun Day?"

Mrs. Martin looked at me, paused, and then frowned. "Why, yes," she said. "Yes, I did say that. How kind of you to remind me." She turned toward Hollis and added carefully, "I'm afraid, Hollis, that you'll have to sit out of tomorrow's Fall Fun Day."

Hollis's smile faded. She nodded at Mrs. Martin and then turned to take her seat. As she past me, she flashed me a look so cold it made me shiver. I took a deep breath and braced myself. She was going to get even with me. No doubt about it. The only question was *when*. And *how* …

Language class droned on and on. I was so tired from my weekend adventures that I nearly fell asleep. I perked up just as Health class began. Mrs. Martin explained that we were to begin a project on substance abuse. As luck would have it, we were allowed to work in pairs.

I loved working in pairs because I had Paula-Jean and she had me. Ever since kindergarten, we always teamed up for stuff. I really felt sorry for some kids, like Jason Jenkins. He was always left standing on his own. Jason's problem was that he was a fanatic when it came to assignments. He'd do life-sized, 3-D models, write fifty pages, research dozens of books, and, worst of all, force his partners to do the same. Keeping up with Jason was impossible, so no matter how hard you worked, your end of the project always paled in comparison and you ended up with a lousy mark. No one wanted to be partners with Jason. No one.

"Okay," said Mrs. Martin. "Choose your partner and then sit down with them to start to work on your pre-writing organizer."

She'd barely finished her last word, when chaos erupted. Everyone darted this way and that. I, however, stood firmly in my place, secure in the knowledge that

Paula-Jean would be arriving shortly and we'd sit together at my desk to work. I yawned and stretched, mildly amused at the frenetic scene, when suddenly I realized something was off. Paula-Jean hadn't arrived. I scanned the class and caught sight of her still sitting at her desk.

Then it all unfolded before my eyes like some warped slow-motion movie. I watched in horror, as Hollis moved swiftly and deliberately toward Paula-Jean. I stood up and lurched forward, but it was too late. Hollis had already passed, casting a narrow-eyed glance at me before smiling warmly at Paula-Jean. Her puckered pink lips were moving. I knew exactly what she was saying. But it was like I was in some sort of horrific nightmare where the classroom stretched longer and longer and I couldn't make it to them in time.

"Sure," Paula-Jean was saying just as I arrived at her desk.

"Perfect," said Hollis. "Just perfect."

The two sat down side by side, leaving me standing, hovering over them like a stray balloon, the expression of utter disbelief frozen on my face.

I don't know how long I was standing there in suspended animation, but when I finally came to my senses and turned around, everyone was sitting.

The entire class.

Everyone.

Except me.

Me and Jason Jenkins, who was walking toward me, grinning and eyeing me like I was a huge hunk of chocolate cake.

Hollis had gotten even with me all right. And what's worse, Paula-Jean had hung me out to dry.

The day couldn't have ended quickly enough. I just managed to hold it together until home time when I threw all my books and lunch bag and junk into my backpack and practically flew down the street.

"Claire!" pleaded Paula-Jean, scrambling to catch up with me. "Please, Claire!"

I stormed straight ahead, refusing to even look at her. I left her standing at the corner, calling after me. I wasn't going to give her the satisfaction of a single word, but then, in a moment of sheer fury, I spun round and hollered as loud as I could.

"Paula-Jean Fanelli, you're as loyal as a sea cucumber!"

I didn't even wait for her reaction. I did an about-face and sprinted the rest of the way home. I made it into my house, slammed the door, and leaned back onto it just as the tears began to fall.

10

Looking back now, I suppose I should have stopped, cooled off, and thought things through. But like Paula-Jean said, I was impulsive by nature. And I was angry. And hurt. And I had a little green book of magic spells just itching to be used. Put it all together and it was a pretty lethal combination. So, to tell you the truth, things could have ended up a whole lot worse than they did.

I dropped my backpack in the hall, ran up to my room, threw myself on my bed, and bawled into my pillow until I was practically dehydrated. I don't know if I was angrier at Hollis or Paula-Jean. Tough to say. All I know is that I felt like the world was a grey, moth-eaten blanket that had just flopped on top of my head.

I was so consumed with anger and hurt that I didn't even think about the book until Cyrus came prancing into my room carrying, of all things, the slightly chewed, very goobery dwarf winterberry euonymus branch. He placed it at my feet like it was some kind of mystic message. I bolted up straight in my bed. An evil grin lit my tear-stained face. Oh, I was going to get even with Hollis for stealing my best friend and making my life miserable, all right. I was going to make her pay.

I swiped the remaining tears from my eyes and sprang from my bed. I stomped past Cyrus and rummaged through my sock drawer, locating my little book in the spot where I'd hidden it. I stared at the cover for a few seconds delighting in the idea of how much power I was holding in my all too eager hands. Then I gently turned the pages, one by one, until I found exactly what I was looking for.

Binding Hex
By the light of the waxing moon, hold a piece of cord. Tie seven knots and pull them tight while chanting three times:

Shut the mouth,
Seal the eyes,
Clasp the limbs,
Tie the ties
Block the ears,
Twist the toe,
Hold the heart,
Bind my foe.
No longer canst thou cause me harm,
By notion, word or deed,
Until thought, word or deed with kindness be done,
With knots, I shall bind thee.

That night, I lay in bed counting the minutes until midnight. The *witching hour* had worked for me so far, so I figured, why mess with a good thing? Luckily, the moon was once again on my side — it was waxing its little way into the night sky.

I'd pulled a lace off my old running shoe and was twisting it round and round my finger under my covers. At the stroke of midnight I began the curse, making sure to tie each knot carefully and chant the words as best I could remember them. When I was done, I held the lace up to my face. A sliver of moonlight snuck through the blinds setting all seven knots aglow.

"There. That ought to do it." I stifled a giggle. "Hollis Van Horn, consider yourself officially hexed!"

Cyrus nudged open my bedroom door. He lumbered his old, overweight body toward me, but before he lay down beside my bed, he poked my shoulder with his wet snout. He let out a low gurgle. I don't know if it was my guilty conscience, but it really sounded like he was telling me off.

"But she deserves it, Cyrus," I whined. "She went too far. She stole Paula-Jean from me. Paula-Jean!"

Cyrus grunted, and then instead of sinking to his usual spot beside me, he turned and waddled back out of my room. I imagined him shaking his little head, *tsk, tsk, tsk*, as he left.

"Dumb dog," I hissed. I flipped over and yanked the covers over my head. Hollis Van Horn brought this on herself, I rationalized. She totally asked for it.

I must have slept soundly, because the next thing I knew, it was morning. I rubbed my eyes and stretched, swung my legs around the side of the bed, and sat up. I yawned deeply. I ruffled through my sheets and covers, but for some strange reason I couldn't locate my knotted shoelace. I pulled the covers completely off my bed and shook them violently. Nothing.

Huh, I thought. *That's weird*. Maybe it was the fact that I'd slept soundly for the first time in several days, but I felt refreshed, almost lighthearted. It didn't seem to matter that I'd lost my shoelace. I shrugged, figuring it would turn up. And no biggie if it didn't.

That morning, I totally expected Paula-Jean to be waiting for me at the corner. When I saw that she wasn't there, I dragged my feet, walking as slowly as I possibly could while still maintaining forward motion. I figured she must be late and since I didn't want to be caught actually standing around waiting for her, I went super slow, even stopping several times to scrutinize an anthill, reorganize my backpack, and fix the ponytail restraining my frizzy mop. When I reached the corner, I looked up and down the street. No Paula-Jean. Refusing to believe she'd gone on without me — an utterly absurd idea — I decided she must be sick or something. I actually began to worry about her — poor thing, must have pneumonia or worse — so imagine my shock when I stepped into the schoolyard and saw Paula-Jean not only standing there, but hanging around with the gargoyles! I was so focused on Paula-Jean and her complete and absolute betrayal that I failed to notice that Hollis was nowhere to be found. I glared at Paula-Jean as I clumped past her, and though I'm sure she must have seen me out of the corner of her eye, she didn't even have the decency to look at me and give me the satisfaction of allowing my scowl to bother her. What nerve!

It was only when Mrs. Martin was calling out attendance that I noticed for the first time that Hollis's seat was empty.

"Has anyone seen Hollis this morning?" asked Mrs. Martin.

I almost laughed out loud when her friends all chimed in.

"Nope," said Tiffany.

"Not me," said Tenisha.

"I think she's sick," said Cheyenne.

Okay. I know this sounds cruel, but I was happy about it. I really was. I'd cursed Hollis and here she was away from school, sick. A plethora of vile images flitted through my brain, and I'd be lying if I said I wasn't relishing every single one. I imagined Hollis sneezing and coughing — her nose as purple and swollen as a rutabaga. Then I pictured her itching and aching, crying out in desperate agony. Maybe her beautiful blond hair had turned granny-grey. Or maybe her pretty little feet had gone all warty and hobbit-like. Or maybe she was covered in green blotches or crusty scabs. I let my imagination run maliciously wild.

I felt so great that I hardly even minded when I had to move to sit beside Jason Jenkins to work on our health project. I almost thanked him when he handed me the thousand-page textbook titled *The History and Health Hazards of the Tobacco Industry From the 1500s to the Present Day* that he wanted me to read for research. It was like I was a pink balloon, floating high in the air, and nothing could drag me down.

Nothing, that is, except Paula-Jean. She sure popped my balloon and sent me plummeting back to reality when Mrs. Walker offered her the opportunity to join another group and she went and picked Tenisha Brown instead of me! Tenisha of all people! Tenisha was Hollis's best friend! I gritted my teeth and counted to seven thousand. I wouldn't let Paula-Jean get to me. No way. I was going to enjoy my Hollis-free day even if it was the last thing I did.

That afternoon was Fall Fun Day. There were tons of great events like Catch the Cucumber, Dodging Doughnuts, and Chuck the Chicken. My favourite events, of course, were the races. I was the fastest girl in my grade, so I was always guaranteed a ribbon or two.

It bothered me that I was on my own and that Paula-Jean was suddenly all BFF with Tenisha and Tiffany and Cheyenne, but when it came to the races, it didn't matter. I was going to clean house.

I stood at the starting line of the hundred-metre. The sky was a perfect shade of powder-blue. Though the air was crisp, the afternoon sunshine gave an illusion of warmth. I took a deep breath and the musky scent of fall leaves and damp earth filled my nostrils.

"Runners, take your mark," announced Mrs. Walker, who was marshalling the races. "Get set. GO!" She fired a fake pistol into the air and before the sound had time to travel from the gun to my ears, I was halfway across the field, my little legs scurrying toward the finish line like my feet were on fire.

Then it happened.

All of a sudden, I felt myself going down. My feet stuck together like they were caught in a net. My hands flew forward to brace myself for the fall. I hit the ground hard and skidded to a halt, my hands and cheek sliding across the grass and dirt. I looked up just as the other girls flew past me and when the last one was gone, my feet broke apart as though someone had just cut the invisible wire attaching them.

Though I was devastated at not winning the ribbon, I tried to make light of the incident, chalking it up to a weird cramping of the foot or perhaps some obstacle in my path. But when the exact same thing happened during the two-hundred-metre and the four-hundred-metre, I decided that something was definitely wrong.

I gave up on racing and tried catching the cucumber, but my fingers seized up at the last second and the darn vegetable smacked me on the shin. Next I lined up to chuck the rubber chicken. Feeling fairly confident, I wound up for the throw, but somehow the chicken slipped through my fingers, flying backward out of my grasp, and striking the principal, Mr. Liew, right in the face. Everyone burst into fits of laughter. Everyone except Mr. Liew and me, that is. I couldn't control my own body and it was starting to make me a bit nervous.

Aside from the fact that I didn't get one single ribbon, I was also suddenly the laughingstock of the whole school. When Paula-Jean passed me to pick up a rubber chicken, I wondered whether she would make some kind of snide comment, but she didn't. Without so much as a sideways glance, she just chucked her chicken at the bucket. I purposely stepped right in her path while she was heading to the back of the line and caught her eye for a fraction of a second before she sidestepped me. Maybe it was wishful thinking, but I thought I saw something resembling regret there — or was it pity? Either way, I opened my mouth to say something to her, but my tongue twisted up and all that came out was, "Blah."

Paula-Jean kept walking as though she hadn't heard.

11

Two more days passed without Hollis at school, and by Friday, I have to tell you I was getting a titch worried — not about her, mind you, but about me! I'd been stumbling and fumbling and bumbling and mumbling the entire time. I'd tripped over my own feet countless times. I'd walked into walls, dropped pencils, utensils, not to mention my mother's best crystal vase. My ears felt like they were plugged and my eyes prickled, forcing me to blink exorbitantly. Despite all the warning signs, it wasn't until my project presentation with Jason Jenkins that it became clear to me what I was up against.

"Jason and Claire," announced Mrs. Martin, after thanking Paula-Jean, Tenisha, and Tiffany for their riveting presentation using a combination of poetry and tableau to demonstrate several strategies to counter the pressures to smoke, drink, and take drugs.

As Jason unveiled a model of a healthy human lung he'd whipped together using balloons, surgical tubing, a three-way hose connector, and modelling clay, I felt my tongue begin to swell. I tried to chew it back down to size while Jason demonstrated the healthy lungs, but that only made it swell all the more. Next, Jason opened a jar filled with a black tar-like substance and, using a funnel, he poured the gunk into a balloon to show the class what smokers' lungs look like and how they are unable to function properly. I was sure my tongue was the size of a lemon when Jason turned the presentation over to me. I took a deep breath and cleared my throat.

"Moking ih maa," was all I managed to get out.

Mrs. Martin's face contorted. "I beg your pardon?"

I took another deep breath and tried again. "Moking ih maa mor moo. Ih may moo ick."

"Is there something wrong, Claire?" Mrs. Martin frowned. "Is this supposed to be part of your project or are you trying to develop an accent again, because I suggest ..."

I shook my head violently. "My ongue. My ongue ih wolen."

I held up my part of the project — a poster I'd sketched the night before of a hippopotamus sitting down and squashing a cigarette. It had a caption that read: BUTT OUT! I smiled weakly.

Clearly, Mrs. Martin was unimpressed. She scribbled furiously in her assessment binder and then asked me to go get a drink of water and sit down. "*Your* part of the project was fabulous, Jason — definitely level 4," I heard her say as I exited the class.

"Ason Enkins," I muttered to myself. I knew whatever I said or did would pale in comparison to that overachieving grade-hog. I was almost beginning to wonder what curse I could toss his way, when I came face to face with a portrait of Hollis holding up last year's Spelling Bee award.

Hollis.

The hex.

That was it.

I gasped and held my throat as I stared at Hollis's glistening eyes and sweet smile. I swear she was laughing at me. There was no doubt left in my mind. I'd cursed Hollis pretty good and the darned spell had definitely bounced back *returning to me threefold,* if not three thousandfold. Paula-Jean would have the biggest I-told-you-so party if she ever found out. But she wasn't going to find out. As I bent to take a long drink from the fountain and cool my swelling tongue, my brain switched gears in a flash and I had a new plan. I was going to fix things and fix them immediately. I was going to undo the curse and then *presto!* — both Hollis and I would be back to normal.

That evening, I turned my bedroom upside down searching for the missing knotted shoelace, but it was nowhere to be found. I searched the entire house, racing from one room to another, rummaging through drawers, looking underneath sofa cushions, checking every corner and crevice at least ten times.

My father caught hold of me on one of my journeys through the living room.

"Slow down, Claire," he said, grabbing hold of my shoulders.

"Please, Dad, let go," I huffed. "I'm really busy. I need to find something."

"Take a deep breath and relax. Where you are going is more important than how fast you get there."

"GAH!" I cried. "Not another one of your sayings! Please, Dad, I don't have time to do something as trivial as think."

"Ah, but isn't that your trouble?" He smiled and released me from his grip. He patted me on the back and sat down to watch a *CSI* rerun.

He was right. I didn't take time to think. That's what had gotten me in this mess in the first place. I gave up looking for the shoelace. I had to face the facts — it was gone.

Despondent, I trudged back up to my bedroom. I flipped through my little green book a hundred times, but I couldn't locate any kind of counter-curse. I reread the binding hex over and over, but it gave me no clue as to how to undo the spell. That night I tossed and turned (falling out of my bed several times, I might add). How was I going to get myself out of this mess? How was I going to un-hex (or was it de-hex?) Hollis?

I called Hollis's house on Saturday morning. Her mother answered and said Hollis was unable to come to the phone. Panic rippled through my whole body. Oh what had I done to her? Was she so feeble she couldn't even come to the phone!

"No." I shook my head, refusing to believe what every cell in my body was screaming out at me. "It can't possibly be. I couldn't possibly have that much power. It's the pageant," I told myself. "She must be all wrapped up practising for that dumb pageant."

I decided I had to see for myself. I told my mother I desperately needed to go to the Boxgrove fair. I couldn't live if I didn't see the Miss Teen Turnip Pageant. I could tell by the look on her face that my mother wasn't buying it. She knew I had no use for beauty pageants, but before she could interrogate me further, Jordan offered to go with me and sit through the entire thing (for purely selfish reasons, of course). Reluctantly, my mother agreed to drive us there and pick us up.

I sat impatiently, fidgeting with my chipped nails, watching as candidate after candidate appeared from behind the stage curtain. Most were older than Hollis and I, but some were younger. All were a thousand times prettier than I was. Hollis had to show, I kept telling myself. She had to. When they finally called out her name and she was a no-show, I was so devastated that I practically withered into a heap on the floor.

"She wouldn't miss this pageant for anything," I told myself. "She has to be really sick. Oh, what have I done to her? How am I going to fix this?"

I left the fair completely disheartened, dragging my feet, and only stumbling once or twice. Jordan, on the other hand, had a bounce in his step. He'd managed to get the beauty pageant winner's phone number and was more cheerful than usual.

"You look like crap, Claire," he said, stuffing his face with caramel corn. "Been eatin' that garlic-y oatmeal junk again?"

"No," I sighed. "If you really must know, I cursed somebody using string and knots and now I'm cursed, too, and I have no idea how to undo a rotten curse because my little green book of witch spells failed to include that apparently important information. That's all."

"Oh," said Jordan, shoving another fistful of caramel corn into his mouth as though he hadn't heard a word I'd said. He offered me the bag. "Want some?"

I rolled my eyes and shook my head. It was no use talking to Jordan. What did he know about hexing? And what did he care about me or my problems, anyway? He'd probably be happy thinking it was some kind of joke to watch me stumble my way through life.

I just had to think of something, but I was at a complete loss. I needed help. But who could I turn to? *Who?*

12

"Hey," I said, trying to sound as casual as possible just to gauge whether or not Paula-Jean would even talk to me.

"Hey."

She actually responded, which was a good sign, because for a second there I thought she was going to hang up on me. Still, her voice was flat — almost expressionless.

"So, er, how are you doing, Peej?"

I tried hard to sound upbeat. Peppy. Downright jovial. There was a long pause. I was thinking she might start yelling at me any second. After all, things hadn't exactly been good between us lately and I can't say I didn't deserve a good verbal thrashing. But instead, Paula-Jean let the silence dangle between us like the blade of a guillotine. When she finally spoke, her words came down swift and sharp. To tell you the truth, I couldn't really blame her.

"Why do you want to know? Did you cast some sort of evil curse on me or something?"

Ouch. That hurt. But since it was entirely possible, I decided to let the comment slide.

"No. No, I didn't do *that*, but well, you see, I ... I ..."

"Come on, Claire. Spit it out. I haven't got all day. Is my hair going to fall out? Will I be plagued with dandruff? Attacked by arthritis?"

I had been agonizing over my situation for some time now, bottling up all my anguish and fear, and when Paula-Jean opened the door with her question, it was like everything I'd packed in me came gushing out in a giant tsunami of emotion.

"Oh Paula-Jean, I put this teensy-weensy binding curse on Hollis and now she's off sick and it's all my fault because I was so mad at her for being your partner and taking you away from me because you're my only friend — you're all I've got — and she knew it and she wanted to hurt me because I'd made her miss Fall Fun Day and then I wanted to hurt her back, so I put the curse on her and now she's sick, she's really sick and it's all my fault and I can't undo the spell because I can't find the shoelace and I can't undo the knots and now Hollis is going to be sick forever, maybe even die, because of me and you were right, you were totally right, the book is evil, EVIL, I tell you, and I'm … a … I'm a … a H-HORRIB-BLE P-PERS-SON!"

The last few words sputtered out between fits of hysterical sobs. When I was done, I didn't even try to stop the tears that streamed down my face like a river of regret. My tongue flapped and I gasped and gurgled for several minutes until I managed to get control of myself. I wiped my eyes and nose with my sweatshirt all the while wondering if Paula-Jean was still on the line.

"Y-you s-still there?" I stammered.

"Yep," said Paula-Jean.

"A-are y-you s-still my f-friend?"

"Yep," said Paula-Jean, though I wished she'd have used a more convincing tone.

"W-what are we g-going to do, Peej?" I asked.

"*We*?" Paula-Jean said coolly. "*We*? You have some nerve."

"Go on and say it," I whimpered. "I deserve it. Say *I told you so*."

"Okay. I told you so. There. That doesn't solve any-thing, Claire."

"Does it at least make you feel better?"

"Minimally."

"Look, Peej, I need to undo this curse. I tied seven knots in a shoelace and now I can't find the shoelace to undo them. If I can't undo them, Hollis and I will be cursed forever."

"Oh. So this is about *you*, Claire."

"Well. Sort of. Kind of. But it's more about Hollis. I swear. I really need to remove the curse. I want her to be well again. Honestly. So, what am I going to do? I know you'll think of something, Peej. You always do."

"Not a chance. You got yourself into this mess, Claire, and now you're going to have to get yourself out of it. Even if I wanted to help you I couldn't. Last I checked I wasn't a witch! I told you not to mess with that voodoo stuff, to heed the warning. Remember the warning? The one you so irresponsibly ignored? The one you said was only there so that people didn't sue the publisher?"

"Yes. The publisher. They ought to be sued. The publisher and the ..." I began, but the remaining words died back into my throat when I realized what I was saying.

The warning. The publisher. The author. The author was a witch. A White Witch. She had to know how to undo the curse. It was so simple I kicked myself for not thinking of it right away.

"You're a genius, Peej!" I shrieked. "I knew you'd help me figure a way out of this mess!"

"Whoa!" said Paula-Jean. "I didn't ..."

"Ah, but you did! You did!" I shouted. "Thank you so much, Paula-Jean. You're the best — the very best and I mean it!"

"But, Claire ..."

"No buts — you are!" I said confidently. "I know exactly what I have to do now, Peej. I'm going to fix this. You'll see. I'm going to de-hex Hollis and me and make everything right. And I promise I'm going to be a far less vengeful person in the future. Really."

"Claire ..."

"There's just one teensy-tiny simple thing, Peej," I said tentatively.

I heard Paula-Jean huff, like she was expecting me to ask her to fly to Rome or something. "Are you kidding me? Nothing is ever teensy or tiny or simple with you, Claire."

"It's no biggie. Really," I insisted. "If I just *happen* to be away from school tomorrow and Mrs. Martin just *happens* to ask, can you just tell her I'm sick?"

I could almost hear the *drip, drip, drip* of sarcasm as Paula-Jean spoke. "Oh sure, Claire. I can tell her I think you're sick. And it wouldn't be a lie, since I truly do believe you are sick — in the HEAD!"

"I deserve that, Peej. I do. But can you just file the insults for the moment and promise me ..."

Paula-Jean sighed. "I sure hope you know what you're doing."

"Oh I do!" The words bubbled out of me. "I really do this time, Peej. No worries."

"Why is it when you say *no worries* that I begin to worry?"

"Aw, that's so sweet of you, Peej. You're worried about me!"

I hung up the phone feeling happier than I had in days. Paula-Jean was my friend again and I was going to set the world right. I headed straight for my little green book. This time I knew what I was doing. I really did. Even when I tripped and jammed my toe, I barely even let out a cry.

I opened the book to the copyright page. All it said was:

I frowned. I don't know what I expected to find, but certainly a little more than this. At least I knew it was a local publisher — finding their address wouldn't be difficult, but what I'd really hoped for was some way to contact the White Witch. The wheels in my brain cranked into full gear. "Hmmm … this is going to be a bit trickier than I thought."

13

The digital alarm clock read 5:22 a.m. when I skulked into Jordan's room. Cyrus was stuck to my heels like gum on my shoe, but rather than try to get rid of him and risk waking my parents, I gave him a severe look, which he may or may not have seen, and let him follow me.

"Jordan," I whispered, approaching the snoring pile of jumbled covers.

He didn't stir.

"Jordan," I tried again, this time a bit louder and with a greater sense of urgency. He shifted positions and mumbled something that sounded like *pass the relish*, but he didn't open his eyes.

Frustrated, I leaned in closer and whispered as loudly as I could without breaking into a full-blown scream, "Jordan! Wake up! I need to talk to you!"

This clearly startled him. He sat bolt upright, limbs flying in all directions. Our heads whacked. I heard him swear and Cyrus yelp as I fell backward, tripping over the poor beagle and breaking my fall in Jordan's pile of dirty laundry. A searing pain spread from my skull downward throughout my body.

"Are you nuts, Claire?" Jordan shouted, once he'd

shaken enough sleep to realize what was happening. "What the heck are you doing in my room?"

"I-I …" was all I could get out before he cut me off.

"Get outta here!" he thundered. "Right now or I'll …"

"But Jor —"

"Get lost, Claire, or I swear …"

I scrambled out of the stinky pile of grimy socks and sweaty T-shirts and who knew what else, passed Cyrus, who must have been dazed and confused, to Jordan's bedside and hugged his cheesy-smelling feet. "Please, Jordan," I sobbed. "Please! I need your help. I can't do this without you! Pleeeeaaase!"

He kicked his feet loose from my tight embrace. With what little light there was from the nearly full moon creeping into the room from between the slats in the blinds, I could make out his dark silhouette. He was rubbing his forehead. He grunted a few times and muttered several nasty words under his breath. Finally he addressed me and maybe it was my imagination, but I thought his tone had softened somewhat.

"What exactly is your problem? You've been acting weirder than usual lately."

I inhaled deeply. I had to choose my words carefully or he'd not only kick me out, he'd tell Mom and Dad for sure. I had already tried to tell him about the curse, but that hadn't gotten me very far so I decided to be a bit cryptic this time. I began cautiously, sniffling in between sentences for dramatic effect.

"I need your help, Jordan. I have to do something really important today and I need you to help me skip school. If you call in sick for me, no one will question it — you sound exactly like Dad on the phone. Paula-Jean will back me up, too, so no one — not the school secretary, not Mrs. Martin, not Mom or Dad — no one will know I'm not where I'm supposed to be."

Jordan yawned and stretched. I heard his bed creak with movement. He didn't say anything for the longest time — it took Jordan a long time to think about challenging things.

"Skip school, eh?" he said finally. It was almost like the idea intrigued him. "What are you gonna do?"

He hadn't said no yet. It was a good sign.

"Let's just say, the less you know the better ..."

Jordan sighed and I couldn't tell if it was out of pain or frustration. "Claire, you're not some secret agent or international spy. No one is going to torture me for answers ..."

He did have a point. I'd have to divulge a little more information.

"Okay. I'm just going into the city, is all. I'm going to see a publisher about a book. It's a life-or death-situation. That's all I'm gonna say and it's the truth."

Once again Jordan fell silent. He rubbed his forehead again and swung his legs round the side of his bed mumbling under his breath. My heart sank. There was no way he was going to help me. Not a chance. It was the stupidest idea I'd ever had. What was I thinking? El Doofus Rat Murphy — help *me*? Ludicrous. More likely he'd tell Mom and Dad and delight in my punishment. Paula-Jean was right; I ought to have my head examined.

marina cohen

I reached over and gave Cyrus a gentle pat on the head and a rough scratch behind the ear and then hauled myself to my feet prepared to leave his room empty-handed or worse.

"Never mind —" I began to say, but at the same time Jordan spoke. I stopped dead in my tracks. I swung round to face him. I wasn't quite sure if I'd heard correctly so I added quickly. "What? What did you just say?"

"I said, okay," Jordan muttered.

I shook my head and then stuck a finger in my ear to make sure it wasn't plugged again. I couldn't believe what I was hearing. Jordan was going to help me. He was actually going to help me. My universe was suddenly upside down.

"Grab my cell," he said, "I'd better call now while Mom and Dad are still asleep. I'll leave a message."

I nodded vigorously, keeping my mouth shut — I didn't want to risk saying anything that might tip the already rickety ship. I groped around Jordan's desk for his cellphone and locating it, I passed it to him. Still only half believing this was actually happening, I whispered the school's phone number and listened in sheer amazement as he left the message. It was perfect — he sounded very convincing. I wanted to hug him or something, but figured that might tick him off, so I sort of bowed and muttered a sincere thank you as I turned to leave.

"Hey, Claire."

I froze. My heart leaped into my throat. I knew it was too good to be true. He'd changed his mind. Maybe he was going to yell, "Just kidding!" Or maybe something more sinister — like he was planning to extort money from me. I slowly turned to face my brother, preparing for the worst.

"Here," he grunted, tossing me his cell. I missed and it whacked my shin. He was assaulting me with his phone now! An all-time low. I scrambled to pick it up and throw it back at him, but luckily before I could get my rubbery hand to co-operate he added, "Better take my cell if you're going into the city alone."

I was so stunned that a good sneeze could have knocked me over. Just when I thought I had Jordan totally figured out, he goes and does something this nice. Like he actually really cares about me or something. An awkward silence hung like a curtain between us. I suddenly felt incredibly guilty for magically thrashing him the other night. What could I say to him? How could I apologize and thank him at the same time? I was trying to think of how to phrase it, but luckily he spoke first.

"Now get out of here," he said.

Still in shock, I left his room, holding his cell and shaking my head. Over my shoulder I heard him mutter, "I'm getting a lock put on my door."

14

I was riddled with guilt when my mom kissed me on the cheek, smiled gently, and wished me a good day. Cyrus was sitting at the door, back straight, his snout pointing accusingly at me. I hung my head and kept my eyes trained on the ground, trying to conceal my shame as I nudged him aside. I was absolutely certain that deceit was scribbled all over my face in some bright neon colour. *Liar! Liar! Pants on fire!* My jeans were definitely smouldering.

I hated being dishonest — especially with my parents. They were good parents and they always encouraged me to tell the truth, no matter what the consequences. I could hear my father as clear as day, cautioning me, "Oh, what a tangled web we weave, when first we practise to deceive, ..." For a second I considered coming clean and telling him the whole story. Trouble was, he wouldn't believe me. I mean what adult in their right mind would? "What an imagination, Claire," he'd say, patting me on the head. "Now off you go, and try not to curse anybody else at school today." Maybe he'd even come up with one of his sayings. *Curse me once, shame on you ... curse me twice, blah, blah, blah.*

No. I couldn't tell my parents. This was my mess

and Paula-Jean was right. I needed to clean it up all on my own. Well, *sort of* on my own.

I skulked in the shadows of the park across the street from the huge home until the last car left the driveway. I watched the black Mercedes drive down the street and turn at the lights. When I was certain it wasn't coming back, I made my move.

I rang the doorbell once and waited. When no one answered, I tried again. I waited an entire minute (I know, because I counted. One Mississippi. Two Mississippi. Three …). Then I began pounding on the door. Still, no one answered. I continued to hammer my knuckles against the solid wood door, while my mind raced. Was Hollis even at home? Had they taken her to a hospital? Was she lying in some uncomfortable metal-framed bed, connected to oodles of computers, machines, and wires, clinging to sweet life by a tattered and fraying thread? *Stay away from the light, Hollis! Stay. Away. From. The …*

The door opened a crack and a bloodshot eye peeped out.

"What do *you* want?" said the pitch-perfect voice as the door swung open all the way revealing a very tired-looking, very pale Hollis. Her eyes had dark circles around them as though she hadn't slept well in days.

To tell you the truth, I was slightly taken aback. I honestly didn't know what to expect (I mean, I *had* imagined the green crusty blotches and hobbit-feet and all, but I hadn't been serious about that). So when I saw Hollis standing in front of me looking sick and fragile, the reality of my curse really hit home. This was beyond my expertise, I decided. This was going to take more than a giant bowl of yogurt and a few handfuls of chopped garlic. Good thing I had a plan.

I stood for a second wondering how to explain to Hollis what I'd done. How could I phrase it so that she didn't think I was some kind of raving lunatic? Check. She already *did* think I was a raving lunatic — so I gave up and decided to just come clean and let the chips fall where they may.

I'd actually wanted to begin by saying *I cursed you*, but figures, my tongue got all tangled, and what came out was simply, "Curse you."

I winced as Hollis's perky little nose wrinkled in disgust.

"Look, Claire," she huffed. "I'm sick. I don't have time to listen to your insults —" She began to close the door.

"I know you're sick," I interrupted, pushing the door back open. "*I'm* the reason you're sick. I meant to say *I cursed you*, and —"

"Go away, Claire!" she said. "I'm not kidding. I'm not feeling well and I'm not in the mood for your ridiculous stories. Besides, shouldn't you be at school annoying Mrs. Martin and the rest of the class?" She tried closing the door again, but she was weak and I was stronger. I held it open.

"Please listen to me, Hollis. I know you hate me — I don't know *why* you hate me — but I know you do and I'm not here about that or anything crazy — well, it is sort of crazy, but that's beside the point. I bought this little book at the grocery store ..." I grappled in my pocket, pulled out my green book and practically shoved it in her face. "See? It's a book of spells and I cursed you because you asked Paula-Jean to be your partner and I got stuck with Jason. Now you're sick and it's all my fault and I'd fix it if I could. I swear, Hollis. But I don't know how. You have to believe me, because I have a plan and I'm going to make you better — you'll see. You just have to believe me."

She glowered at me for a second, like she thought I was purposely trying to antagonize her, but then I added, "Please."

Maybe it was the sincerity of that last word or maybe it was the tears pooling in my eyes. Or maybe she was just too weak to argue. At any rate, she released the door. She looked me up and down. "Come on in," she said finally. She turned and walked calmly toward the living room. I shut the door and scurried after her.

Hollis's house was as perfect as she was. Polished marble and hardwood floors, huge baseboards and crown mouldings, heavy brocade drapes, and nothing — not one thing — looked out of place. Even the books that were strewn across the coffee table looked like they'd actually been arranged to look strewn. *Wow*, I thought to myself. *It's like this house is some kind of show home. Barely looks lived in.* My mother would be pea-green with envy. She was always going on about how hard she worked to keep our house tidy and how between Jordan, Cyrus, and me, the house constantly looked like a tornado had ripped through it.

Hollis sat down on the edge of the sofa, like she was worried she might crinkle the fabric. She looked at me with her sea-foam eyes. She was wearing pink silk paja-mas — with a matching headband, for crying out loud! It killed me — even sick as a dog, Hollis still managed to look stunning.

I lowered myself into a chair opposite her and cleared my throat. "Listen," I said, "I know this is asking a lot — even for me — but I swear it's the truth. I was really angry. I didn't know what I was doing."

Okay. That was only partially true. I did know what I was doing when I cursed Hollis, but I didn't fully understand the consequences of my actions, I rational-ized. I certainly wasn't aware that Hollis would get this ill and that the curse would bounce back on me.

"This book is magic," I said holding it up again for her to see. "It really is. It cured my zit and beat up my brother. If you don't believe me, just go ask Paula-Jean. But, er, don't blame her — I did all the hexing — she was an innocent by-hexer."

Hollis rolled her eyes and sighed. She didn't believe a word I was saying. I decided to try showing her the spell. I opened the book and passed it to her. "Read it," I said.

Hollis took the book in her right hand. For the first time, I noticed her left hand hung limp by her side. I watched her eyes move down the page. Her face remained expressionless. She handed the book back to me.

"You see," I said. "It's the curse. I cursed you. But guess what? The curse bounced back and cursed me, too!" I grinned at her and nodded. I thought she'd be happy about that, but her eyes narrowed. "Seriously," I added. "I've had trouble controlling my body — even my tongue!"

Hollis began to laugh and the tiniest spark lit her eyes.

"What's so funny?" I asked, almost chuckling myself.

"You are, Claire," she said. "You *always* have trouble controlling your tongue."

The smile plummeted from my lips. Hollis was feeling better all right. Better enough to start insulting me again.

"I'm not here to argue with you," I said.

"Then why *are* you here?" she asked.

"To help you, of course," I said, like it was the most obvious thing in the world. "To de-hex you!"

Hollis leaned back into the sofa. She looked away for a second and when she looked back she was crying. Her voice trembled and I couldn't tell if it was with anger or fear.

"You didn't curse me," she said. "There's something really wrong with me. I get these awful headaches and I get dizzy and now my left side is numb. The doctors haven't been able to find out what's wrong with me yet. I'm scheduled for more tests tomorrow. So, as much as I'd love to blame you, Claire …"

"Blame me! Blame me!" I shouted. I got off the chair and rushed to her side on the sofa. "Hollis, please believe me! I did this to you! I really did!"

She swiped at her eyes and glared at me.

I decided to try a different approach. "Okay, okay," I said. "Fine. I didn't curse you. You got sick all on your own. But … what if I did? What if I really caused whatever is wrong with you? Wouldn't you want to just try and let me de-hex you? I mean, what have you got to lose?"

"Besides my sanity?" she said dryly.

I frowned.

"Nothing, I guess." Her voice was quiet. Resigned.

"So let me do this," I said quickly, before she had time to change her mind. "Let me just de-hex you. I just know everything is going to be fine. You'll see."

She stared at me for the longest time. Her expression remained skeptical, but there was something in her eyes that said she hoped I was right.

"Fine," she said. "Go ahead. De-hex me."

"Great!" I shouted. "Perfect! You're not going to regret this!" I stood up and my knee bumped into one of the coffee-table books, knocking the lot of them onto the floor.

Hollis rolled her eyes. "I already do," she growled.

I scrambled to pick up the books and rearrange them, when Hollis added, "So how exactly are you going to de-hex me?"

I'd managed to pick up all the books, but they slipped from my grasp and dropped to the floor again. "Well, now, see, that's a bit of a problem ..."

"Problem?" Hollis asked, sounding confused. She reached down with her right hand and began picking up one book at a time, placing each delicately back into its perfect spot.

"Um, yeah," I said. "I don't really know how to de-hex you ..."

Hollis froze. "*What?*" she said, her voice brimming with disbelief.

"Don't worry," I added reassuringly. "The White Witch knows. And we're going to find her. So go put on some of your fancy designer sweats — I'm taking you into the city."

Luckily the curse hadn't dulled my reflexes too much and I managed to duck the big, fat book that Hollis chucked at me.

15

"Remind me again why I'm doing this?" Hollis said, pulling the door shut and locking it.

"Because you are going to be cured, silly," I said, checking first right, then left, and then yanking her down the steps toward the sidewalk. "You just need to trust me," I said confidently, as I dragged her toward the bus stop.

Hollis lagged behind. I could hear her left shoe scraping along the cement. She seemed to be getting worse. I had to get her de-hexed and quickly. It was nearly ten o'clock. Hollis had taken over half an hour getting ready. I mean, seriously — who puts on makeup to see a *witch*? Even though I totally felt responsible for Hollis's situation, I can honestly say I wasn't exactly enjoying her company. I wanted to get this thing over with as quickly as possible and get my own life and limbs back to normal, so I grabbed onto her jacket sleeve and pulled her along to keep up.

Luckily, before sneaking out of my house, I'd done two things. First, I'd raided my secret cash-stash — the one I'd been saving for a tattoo removal on the odd chance my parents actually let me get a tattoo I'm bound to regret. I had to be prepared. I had amassed a total of forty-five dollars and sixty-two cents — not exactly a fortune, but, hey, the way I saw it, I had at least another decade before I'd be old enough to get one, love it for, oh, say a year, hate it passionately for another two, and then plan its removal. By then, there will be generations of people needing to be de-inked so they'll have most likely invented a cheap and pain-free method, right? That's what I was counting on, anyway. The second thing I did was Google the publisher. I got their address and even a map. This was going to be easy.

"Have you got a bus ticket?" I asked, as the vehicle lurched to a halt in front of us. A puff of noxious fumes caused me to step back before stepping forward.

"Why would *I* have a bus ticket?" Hollis responded, as though it were the most ridiculous question in the world. "I've never taken the bus in my entire life. My mother doesn't believe in public transit — she says it's too *pedestrian*."

Oh brother, I thought. Aside from her totally environmentally unfriendly stance, it was also elitist. But did I expect anything else from the Van Horn family?

I rolled my eyes and reached into my pocket. I got on the bus and dropped two tickets into the fare box. Good thing I had some money — I'd have to buy more tickets for the ride home. I almost started walking down the aisle when I noticed, out of the corner of my eye, Hollis still standing on the curb. I swung round and grabbed her arm and pulled her on board.

"*Threefold*," I muttered under my breath. "More like bounce back *three-million-fold*."

"What's that?" asked Hollis.

"Er, nothing," I said.

As the bus bumped and jostled its way toward the subway station I had to deal with Hollis and her barrage of whiny questions.

"So, where does this White Witch live?" she asked.

"No idea," I said, which apparently caused her all sorts of anxiety.

"What? What do you mean you don't know where she lives?" Hollis yelled.

"Keep your voice down," I said. "Stop attracting attention — I *am* skipping school, remember? And anyway, I told you to trust me — I have a plan."

"Claire Murphy, you are the last person in the world I trust," said Hollis. "And if we're not going to the White Witch, then where exactly are we going?"

"To the publisher of the book," I said, trying to keep my answer as brief as possible so as not to cause her to freak-out any further.

"And where is that?"

"Downtown."

"Where downtown?"

"Queen Street."

"And what do you hope to do at the publisher's? How are they supposed to de-hex me? With ink and erasers?"

"You ask too many questions," I said. "Just trust me. I know what I'm doing."

"Trust you? Trust you! Famous last words …" she scoffed.

I'd had enough Hollis for the moment. I got up and threw myself into the row of seats opposite her. Yes, yes,

yes — I still felt guilty and responsible for her frail condition, and I was going to fix that, but did I have to let her annoy me while I did so? I wished Paula-Jean were with us. Paula-Jean was even-tempered. She would be able to defuse the tension between Hollis and me.

I pretended to look out the window, all the while keeping an eye on Hollis. Her posture wasn't good and she was fidgeting nervously with her left fingertips. I could tell she was uncomfortable sitting there alone, but I decided to let her suffer a little while longer. Then, when a really ragged-looking guy — not much older than Jordan, I guessed — got on the bus, sat down beside her, and started harassing her, I had no choice but to spring into action.

"Leave her alone," I said, racing toward them.

"Get lost," he said.

Hollis looked petrified.

"Do you see this book, buddy?" I said grabbing it out of my pocket and brandishing it like a sword. "This is magic. And believe me I will not think twice about cursing your butt into the next millennium! Now move!"

"Chill, man," he said, waving the book out of his face. He shifted down the row a few seats. "I was only asking if she could spare some change ..."

Satisfied I'd rescued Hollis, I calmed down, tucked my book away, and looked him over. His hair looked like it hadn't been washed in days. His fingernails were dirty and his hands looked way older than his face. So did his eyes, for that matter. He was a street kid. Clearly homeless. I felt bad for threatening to curse him. Apparently,

95

I hadn't learned my cursing lesson yet. I reached into my pocket and before I knew what I was doing, I'd handed him five bucks.

"Thanks," he muttered. Something about the way he said that made me realize it was a fortune to him.

"Why did you do that?" hissed Hollis. "I wouldn't have given that guy a dime!"

I looked at Hollis's fancy clothes and fancy shoes. Her painted nails and expensive earrings. I looked back at the guy who had no one and nothing — nothing except the five bucks I'd just given him. I suddenly found myself wondering if I wasn't the only one who had some *character-cleansing* to do.

16

MIXED PICKLE PRESS was written in chipped gold paint on the window of a small, dingy door wedged between a Persian rug store and a pizzeria. Half of the buildings in the area consisted of modern chi-chi type cafés, furniture stores, and clothing boutiques, while the other half were remnants of darker days. I pressed my face up to the glass. A narrow staircase was visible through the greasy film. I could tell the walls hadn't been painted — or washed, for that matter — in decades.

"You're joking, right?" said Hollis. "You can't possibly expect me to follow you in there? What kind of a publisher is this, anyway?"

I had my own concerns about ascending those stairs, but I wasn't about to let Hollis know that. "Obviously one that isn't doing too well."

She rolled her eyes. "Very funny."

"Come on," I said. "I can't do this without you."

"And why not?"

"Because," I said, reaching for the tarnished brass doorknob, "I can't just walk in there and go demanding to see the White Witch. Do you think publishers just hand out the real names and addresses of their authors

— ones that obviously use pseudonyms for privacy? My plan requires the two of us. So get yourself in here or stay cursed forever."

The threat seemed to do the trick. Hollis narrowed her eyes and motioned. *"Après vous."*

I swung the door open. Its hinges screamed like I was torturing them. I stepped inside, with Hollis at my heels. The stairwell smelled musty — like a hamper full of unwashed clothes. I can't say I wasn't a tad worried, but it was a place of business, I told myself, not some motorcycle gang's hideout.

I took a deep breath and crept up the stairs. Hollis was holding my arm in a death grip. At the top landing I had to turn right. The dank hallway gave way to a space not much larger than my living room. What I saw there melted my fear into a puddle of bewilderment. I scrunched my eyes and opened them. I wasn't dreaming.

An old floral sofa, complete with doilies on the headrests, was off to one side. There was a rickety coffee table with piles of mini books similar to my *Remedies, Rituals, and Incantations* scattered across the top. A few old picture frames adorned the walls — some that looked like they housed certificates or awards. In the opposite corner there were several metal filing cabinets and a huge old wooden desk with a computer that could be politely classified as antique. And sitting at the desk that was covered in piles of manila envelopes of various sizes and shapes, was a rather large, rather menacing-looking clown.

17

Now clowns, at the best of times, can be pretty creepy. But this clown, sitting at his desk, in his dingy office, hammering away at a keyboard as old as my grandma's galoshes, was downright frightening. I have no idea why I didn't do an about-face and burn rubber back down that staircase. It was like my feet had suddenly been disconnected from my brain.

Luckily, the clown was too engrossed in cyberspace to notice the two of us peeping round the corner at him. Was he working? Twittering? Facebooking? I wasn't going to hang around long enough to find out. Behind me, I heard a faint whimpering. Obviously, Hollis had a major clown-aversion, as well. I actually managed to lift one foot and move it slowly backward, but just as I began my careful retreat, wouldn't you know it — Jordan's cellphone rang.

Dun, dun, dun, dun, daaaah … dun, dun, dun, dah, daaaaah …

(Did I mention Jordan has this super-loud, super-annoying ringtone? It's the *Monday Night Football* theme song, for crying out loud!)

Well. That did it. Any chance of escaping the situation unscathed evaporated. The clown looked up, and while I grappled for the phone, he got out of his chair (he had to be almost seven feet tall!) and began moving toward us at a steady pace. My thoughts scattered in a million directions. *Should I run? Should I stay to get what I came for? Should I answer the phone?* I decided on the latter — it made the best sense. If I was going to be attacked by a deranged clown, at least there would be someone on the other end of the phone line to witness it.

"Hello?" I said, my voice squeakingly high.

(The clown was smiling at me. At least I thought he was — tough to tell behind his painted-on grin ...)

"It's me, Jordan."

(Hollis was pulling hard at my jacket. She nearly made me tip backwards.)

"Figures," I said.

(The giant clown was waiting patiently — perhaps to welcome me, or perhaps to bludgeon me — at this point, his motives were unclear.)

"Are you okay?" asked Jordon.

(Hollis was pulling with all her might. Luckily — or unluckily, I suppose — she had no strength in her left arm.)

"Define *okay*," I said.

(The clown waved at Hollis, who, not forgetting proper etiquette, stopped pulling on me long enough to wave back.)

"I'm calling from Mac's phone," said Jordan, oblivious to the clownish mayhem happening on my end. "Call me back at this number, if you need anything, okay?"

"Er, thanks," was all I could think of to say. "I just might need to ..."

I hung up and suddenly, I realized that my world had become a whole heck of a lot more complex. My horrible brother was acting really nice. Clowns were masquerading as regular people. My sworn enemy was hanging onto me for dear life. Nothing made sense. Nothing fit its neat little compartment anymore. My head began to spin.

"Can I help you little ladies?" asked the clown. His voice was calm and friendly — not remotely what one might expect from a deranged clown.

"I, er ... we, well," I stammered. Hollis squeezed me, her long nails digging into my upper arms. It jolted my mouth into action. "We were looking for Mixed Pickle Press."

"Then you've come to the right place!" said the clown. "What can I do for you? Have you written a book? I have to warn you, I'm not actively seeking submissions at this point." He motioned his head toward the staggering pile of manila envelopes polluting his desk.

"Um, no," I said, trying hard to imagine the clown without makeup. Was he old? Young? I couldn't tell. "We were actually looking to gather some information on one of your authors."

"Oh," he said, somewhat surprised. "I see. Hey, aren't you supposed to be in school or something?"

"Er, yes, but ... you see ..." I stammered. "School project," I announced suddenly. It seemed to do the trick.

Meanwhile, Hollis was still cowering behind me. The clown seemed to take notice of her and come to some sort of realization. He looked down at his ballooning orange polka dot pants and his ruffled sleeves. "Oh gosh," he said. "You'll have to excuse my appearance. It's Monday, you know."

I smiled and nodded — the way you do at a toddler who has just said, *eep oble boop*. Like it's supposed to make tons of sense. Was I missing something? Was Monday *clown day* in some bizarre alternate universe?

Sensing my confusion, he began to explain. "Mondays I go to the Hospital for Sick Kids over lunch — to read stories and entertain the children."

Well. You could have knocked me over with a wet noodle. This staggeringly tall clown was not a menace to society — he was a benefit! Hollis let go of my arms and stepped out from behind me, a look of shock plastered across her face. Personally, I was embarrassed. I felt awful for misjudging him. Misjudging people was becoming a reoccurring theme in my life.

"That's pretty nice of you," I said. "I didn't know you could do that sort of thing."

"Oh, there are lots of ways to help out in your community — if you really want to," he said. "Now, tell me, what kind of information were you looking for? Which author?"

Wouldn't you know it? Right then and there my tongue got all twisted up again and all that came out was, "Witch author."

He looked confused. "That's what I'm asking you, which author?"

"Witch author," I repeated.

"What author?"

"Not *what* — witch!" I said.

"Who?"

"Witch! Witch!" My communication frustration was clearly mounting.

Hollis rolled her eyes. "The White Witch," she said calmly, pulling the book out of my pocket and holding it up for him to see.

"Oh," he said, taking the book and turning it over in his hands before passing it back to me. "That's one of my favourites."

"Um, mine, too," I said, untangling my tongue. It wasn't a lie. Despite the trouble the book caused me, I still thought it was pretty cool.

"We need to contact the White Witch," said Hollis. "Can you give us her phone number or something?"

I elbowed Hollis. She'd opened her big mouth and tipped our hand. I had wanted to go about things in an entirely different fashion, way more subtly, but the clown confusion ruined everything.

"No, I can't do that," he said, shaking his rainbow-coloured head. "First off, I don't have the phone number. And even if I did, I couldn't give it to you."

"You don't have your authors' phone numbers?" said Hollis.

"Not that particular one. Very strange, reclusive author, indeed. Just a post office box number," he said. "That's where I send the royalty cheques." He must have thought we looked hopeful because he quickly added, "But I can't give you that either. Privacy, you know. Maybe I can answer your questions?"

"I don't think so," I said, thinking fast. "We need to interview her personally. So, I think we'd best be going now."

"But Claire," said Hollis, at which point I gave her another elbow.

"Gee, that's too bad. Such a shame. Yes, we'll be going na, na, na … NOW!" I said, sneezing the last word out as loudly and as violently as I possibly could. "Excuse me — would you happen to have a tissue?" I swiped at my nose for dramatic effect.

"Sure," he said. For a second I thought he was going to pull out a never-ending string of colourful tissues from his pocket, or something ridiculous like that, but instead, he did exactly what I'd hoped he'd do.

He turned around and headed for a small door at the back of the room. I was sure it was a washroom. As he ducked inside, I made my move. I darted to his desk and grabbed the first item I could find: his coffee cup.

"Have you lost it, Claire?" whispered Hollis. "You're going to steal his mug?"

"Hush!" I snapped, racing back to my original spot, hiding the mug behind my back. "I'm not stealing it! I'm borrowing it!"

Just then, the clown reappeared with a wad of tissue. I held the mug in my left hand and took the tissue with my right, pretending to wipe my nose and then shove it into my pocket. I shook his hand and thanked him for his time. I frowned at Hollis, scrunching one eye more than the other. I hoped she understood my nonverbal attempt at communicating, "Let's get outta here!" I backed up slowly, keeping the mug hidden, all the while grinning and nodding at the clown. Once I reached the landing, I darted around the corner and dashed back down the stairs. I could hear Hollis muttering nasty words and questions all the way down and out the door.

18

"Claire, I always thought you were nuts, but now I'm completely convinced you have serious psychological issues!" said Hollis as soon as the door slammed shut behind us. "You are definitely in need of major therapy! If you needed a cup of coffee that desperately, all you had to do was —"

I stood there grinning ear to ear, dangling the mug by its handle between my thumb and index finger. "For your information," I interrupted, "this mug is going to get us everything we need. And for what it's worth, you are starting to sound like Paula-Jean ..."

Hollis wouldn't have guessed it, but that last part was actually a compliment. She glared at me like she wanted to throttle me — and she may very well have, had curiosity not gotten the better of her. "And how exactly is it going to do that?" she demanded. "Is it going to start talking to us? No, wait. I know. Now you're a psychic and you're going to read our future in the coffee grinds! Or better yet, the mug is going to lead us to the White Witch like some sort of divining rod ..."

I ignored her rant and entered the pizzeria next door. It was nearly lunchtime, after all, and my stomach had been growling forever. Hollis followed me, continuing her tirade. I ordered two pepperoni strombolis and two bottles of water from the kind-looking lady behind the counter. Hollis sure was costing me a lot of money. My tattoo-removal money was dwindling. I'd be stuck with my hypothetical bad ink for a few years longer than I was planning. Maybe I should just stick to temporary tattoos. Or perhaps a nice, conservative tongue-piercing.

All the while, Hollis didn't let up, blathering on and on — something about me being a pathological kleptomaniac — until we were seated in a booth, the coffee cup placed strategically in the centre of the table. She took a bite of her stromboli, apparently appeased for the moment by the hot, gooey cheese, and unwilling to talk with her dainty mouth full. I took the opportunity to get out my little green book and flip through the pages, locating exactly what I was searching for. Hollis and the clown may have stuck a wrench in my original plan, but I had another plan — a better plan. One that involved a little bit of magic.

I passed the book to Hollis just as she was taking a sip of her water. I watched her eyes scan the title, but then the spray of water exploding from her mouth forced me to shut my eyes.

"A spell?" she choked. Her already high-pitched voice reached new altitudes. "You're going to cast a *spell* on the *clown?*"

"Not just *a* spell — *this* spell," I said casually, chewing a hunk of stromboli then dabbing at my face with my paper napkin. "And not *me* — *we*. Need I remind you that you have a vested interest in this mission?" I left the book open in front of her.

We ate the rest of our food in silence. I could tell Hollis was in the middle of some sort of inner struggle. When she was finished eating, she glowered at me defiantly, all the while rubbing her left fingertips with her right hand. She picked up the book up and read the spell out loud.

Charm Spell
1 cup whole wheat flour
1/2 cup of salt
1/3 cup of water

Place the flour in a wooden bowl. Holding the salt in one hand, allow it to slip through your fingers. Pour the water in slowly. All the while chanting:

> *Flour is earth, nourishment, innocence;*
> *Salt is purity, power, protection;*
> *Water is life, desire, emotion.*

Using finger tips, mix ingredients while imagining your intended. Fashion a talisman from the dough. Let dry overnight.

Close your eyes. Clear your mind. While holding a personal belonging of the

intended in one hand and the talisman in
the other, chant the following lines three
times:

Defences destroyed,
Walls worn,
Ramparts rendered,
Shields shorn,
Open thyself to my suggestions
Surrender thy thoughts to my will and intentions.

*Note: Of all spells, charm spells are the
most challenging. They require absolute
concentration. Confused minds cast confused spells.

"Lovely," said Hollis. "Now, tell me again what you
hope to achieve by this ridiculous action?"

"Simple," I said. "I'm going to charm the clown into
giving us the post office box number and any other
information he has on the White Witch."

"Simple," she repeated. "So, er, Ms. Genius, have you
given any thought as to where you're going to get the
ingredients?"

"Pfft!" I scoffed, holding up the salt shaker and
scanning the restaurant. "Need I remind you we're in
a pizzeria?"

"Fine. And you're just going to go up to the counter
and ask for a cup of whole wheat flour."

I smiled at her and stood up. I sauntered up to the counter, exchanged a few pleasantries with the kindly lady, and then returned with two paper cups — a large one containing flour, a small one filled with water.

Hollis shook her head in disbelief. I couldn't tell if she was thoroughly amazed or just plain jealous.

"Okay. So you have flour, salt and water ..."

"Don't forget the clown's personal belonging," I said, tilting my head toward the coffee cup.

"But you're supposed to let the talisman dry overnight. Have you thought about that Ms. Genius? And what about the note — the warning ..."

"Details, shmeetails," I said. "We can't worry about every little thing. We have a charm spell to cast, an address to get, and a witch to see."

I unscrewed the salt shaker and poured the contents in my right hand. A little spilled and, being mildly superstitious, I grabbed a pinch with my left hand and tossed it over my shoulder. Luckily, there was no one seated there. I'd tossed some salt over my left shoulder once and hit Jordan right in the eye. The ensuing episode wasn't pleasant to say the least. I shuddered at the thought.

"Um, Claire," said Hollis. "You'd better hurry. Remember he goes to the hospital over his lunch and it's almost noon."

"Right," I said, picking up the pace and just plopping the remaining salt into the cup, dumping the water in and stirring with one hand to create a pasty dough. All the while I mumbled: "Flour is earth, nourishment, innocence; salt is purity, power, protection; water is life, desire, emotion …"

"Eew. Disgusting," sneered Hollis, as I lifted out my sticky, slimy hand.

I kept on mixing and chanting until I'd formed a mass of dough dense enough to sculpt into a clown.

"There. The legs, the arms, the head …" I said. "*Et voilà!* One talisman ready to go."

"It's not dry, Claire. His arms are drooping and his head is tilting. It looks like it's going to fall off …"

She reached over, but I slapped her hand away. "It's perfect. We don't have any time left, so here." I held the coffee cup in one hand and the talisman in the other and motioned for Hollis to place her hands on them as well. She reluctantly co-operated. "Now close your eyes and clear your mind."

"That should be easy for you," she muttered under her breath.

"Hilarious. Now will you focus and start chanting?"

Anyone looking on must have thought we were luna-tics. I didn't really care — I was getting kind of used to it — but I'm sure Hollis was mortified. I sneaked a peek at her at one point and caught her scanning the restaurant.

"Keep your eyes shut!" I said in the middle of the third round.

"How would you know I had my eyes open unless you had yours open?"

"Stop arguing!" I said, completing the final verse on my own. "Surrender thy thoughts to my will and intentions …"

We both opened our eyes fully and sat staring at one another, still clutching the coffee cup and the drooping talisman that had lost its head during the ceremony.

"This is so not going to work," sighed Hollis.

I raised my eyebrows and grinned. "We'll see about that."

19

You're under my power ... you're under my power ... you're under my ...

With the coffee cup hidden behind my back, I swung open the dingy door and charged up the dark staircase, taking the steps two at a time.

My will and intentions ... my will and intentions ... my will and ...

Hollis was right behind me, huffing and panting and dragging her left foot to keep up. She was sicker than I thought, or seriously out of shape. I hoped it was the latter.

The address of the White Witch ... the address of the White Witch ... the address of the ...

My mind was so focused on charming the clown into giving me the post office box number that I wasn't thinking about anything else when I skittered around the corner at the top of the landing. Wouldn't you know it — the clown was heading around the corner at the exact same time! To avoid bulldozing him, I came to an absolute and abrupt standstill, as did he. Hollis, unaware of my intentions — or the clown's for that matter — continued in forward motion, plowing right into me. Now, I may have been shorter than Hollis, but what I lacked in height I gained in sturdiness. Hollis hit me like a brick wall, falling backward, arms flailing. She landed on her behind with a tumultuous thud.

"Are you okay?" asked the clown, racing to her side and helping her to her feet. In the confusion, I slipped the mug onto the coffee table that was only a few feet away and then rejoined the commotion.

"Are you hurt?" I panted. "Oh my gosh! You're bleeding!" I pointed to a scrape on Hollis's cheek — probably caused by her own long fingernails.

The clown helped Hollis to the sofa, where she sat catching her breath and steadying herself.

"There are some bandages in a first aid kit in the blue filing cabinet," he said to me. "You get the bandage and I'll get a cold compress for her forehead."

I nodded, all the while thinking that her forehead may not be the exact part of her anatomy requiring a cold compress. All the same, I dashed to the back of the room, behind the desk, while the clown disappeared into the bathroom. I yanked open the blue filing cabinet and to my absolute astonishment, I discovered more than just the first aid kit.

Author Information was scrawled on one of the plastic tabs dividing file folders. I couldn't believe my eyes. I'd done it. I'd actually done it. I'd managed to charm the clown into handing me the information I needed! Well, in a roundabout way, I guess.

I momentarily forgot about Hollis and her injury and began rifling through the files at lightning speed. *Turner, Unger, Vanderklaauw (???), White*. That was it! I pulled out the file and opened it. *White, W.* was printed across the top — the White Witch! It had to be her! I quickly memorized as much of the information I could, focusing on the post office box number: 8799 (I memorized this using hockey players — 87 was Sydney Crosby, 99 was Wayne Gretzky — a little trick Jordan taught me ages ago). The postal code was unbelievably easy: L8T 4S2 — it spelled *late for stew!*

"Did you find the bandages?" asked the clown, as he exited the bathroom holding a wad of sopping paper towels.

"Um, yeah," I said, suddenly remembering Hollis. I tucked back the file and fumbled through the first aid kit at the bottom of the cabinet.

"I feel fine," said Hollis. She tried to stand and then sunk back down.

"Do you feel dizzy?" asked the clown, handing her the cold compress.

"Not more than usual," said Hollis.

"She hasn't been feeling well lately," I added. "But don't worry, she's going to be fine — just fine." I winked at Hollis and grinned. I ripped open the bandage and slapped it onto Hollis's cheek, patting it several times to make sure it was on right.

"Ow, quit it!" she said, smacking my hand away.

"Well, that's that. All better," I announced. "We'd best be going now..." I dragged Hollis to her feet, and with one arm around her shoulder, I pulled her toward the door.

"Hold on just a second," said the clown.

I froze. What could he possibly want? Did he figure out I'd taken his coffee cup? Had he discovered I'd been rifling through his files? I was wincing, but he couldn't tell because I had my back to him. I slowly turned to face him, plastering the stickiest-sweet grin on my face that I could possibly muster. I was trying to look cute and innocent, but I think the combination of fear, apprehension, and my crazy huge smile made me look more maniacal than anything. I reached into my pocket to try and use the talisman to charm him again, but unfortunately it was now nothing more than an unidentifiable mass of guck oozing around and sticking to the lining. My mother was going to kill me — but I had a whole half day before I had to worry about that.

"Have you forgotten something?" asked the clown.

What could I have possibly forgotten? I did a quick brain scan. "Um. Nope. Nothing. Thanks again." I turned to leave, but his voice hooked me and reeled me in a second time.

"Are you forgetting what you returned for? Why exactly did you come back?" he asked.

Luckily, my mouth was as fast as a jet engine. It was a shame that my brain was more like a hot-air balloon. "Well," I said sweetly, "we came here about the hospital, of course. You know, to ask you how we could get involved and help out there, too."

Hollis looked at me with a deadpan face. I looked back at her and shrugged. Well, why not? It was as good as excuse as any.

"That's great!" he said. "They can always use people. All you need to do is ..."

"Oh, don't you worry about that," I interrupted. "I'm going to call tomorrow and find out. I'll probably see you there sometime. But right now, I think I need to get my friend home. She's had enough excitement for one day. She's not used to it, you know — rather bland, boring life and all. Besides, Sydney Crosby and Wayne Gretzky are late for stew ..."

Before he could utter any kind of response, and before Hollis could protest, I pulled her toward the hallway and down the steps. I raced along the sidewalk, certain she was only a few steps behind. When we were a safe distance from Mixed Pickle Press, I stopped to catch my breath and explain.

20

"What in the world did you mean?" demanded Hollis.

"Well, you see, Sydney Crosby is number 87 ..." I began, but she cut me off.

"No, no, no!" she shouted. "Not that! About my life! You said my life was boring. And bland. What exactly did you mean by that?"

My eyebrows tangled. Here I'd gotten the address — well, almost the address — of the White Witch and she gets all up in arms about some mindless little commentary. "Oh *thaaat*," I said, rolling my eyes. "It was only an excuse to get us out of there —" I stopped and thought about what I'd said. "But now that you mention it ..."

"Oh. So you *do* think that. You think my life is bland. Boring," she spat. "Well I'll have you know that I happen to lead a pretty exciting life. Way more exciting than your pathetic little existence. Like the beauty pageants I'm in. They are totally exciting — no, thrilling. Yes. My mother says they are thrilling beyond imagination. She says they're suspenseful. And adventurous. And ..."

"Hold on," I said, putting my hand on her shoulder. Now, you'd think I'd have been angry at the *pathetic little existence* crack, but when I looked deep into

her stormy-sea eyes, I saw more than just anger rag-
ing there. I think my comment hurt her somehow.
Really hurt her. And then to make matters worse, I
said something, that in hindsight, maybe I shouldn't
have. Unfortunately I have this horrible habit of speaking first and thinking later. "Seems to me your mother
ought to be in those pageants instead of you if she finds
them so beyond thrilling."

Her eyes were boring holes into my skull as she
shrugged her shoulder away from my hand. If looks
could kill I'd have been reduced to atoms. It was written
all over her face. What I'd said was haunting her. For the
first time, I began to suspect that Hollis didn't like those
beauty pageants half as much as she claimed. Then she
put a hand to her head and squinted and I could tell she
was getting one of her headaches. I had to get her de-
hexed as quickly as possible.

"Come on," I said, my voice a little softer and a little
gentler than usual. "I've got the address. So now all we
need is a post office."

"A post office?" she sighed, her menacing look trans-
forming back to frustration. "Why in the world would
we need a post office if we have the address?"

"Well, because it's not exactly an address," I said,
turning and scouting up and down the street for a drug
store. Drug stores often had post offices within them.
"It's a post office box number, remember?"

She sighed again and began following me up the
street. "Nothing is ever simple with you, is it?" The
venom had left her voice. She no longer loathed and

despised me. She was back to merely hating me. I also wondered if she was beginning to see that complicated could be, well, thrilling.

"Excuse me," I said to a man in a grey suit, hurrying past us. "Do you know where there's a post office around here?"

He stopped long enough to point a long arm toward the opposite side of the street. "Two blocks up. Beside a vintage clothing store."

We walked along the busy sidewalk without saying another word. I was busy crafting my elaborate plan. I had no idea what Hollis was thinking about. Perhaps she was contemplating the latest fashion designs displayed in the shop windows — but I suspected she was still thinking about what I'd said.

The post office was on the far corner, inside a drug store, as I'd suspected. I think Hollis had pretty much resigned herself to the fact that I was, shall we say, a tad unorthodox in my approach to life. All right, she thought I was just plain nuts. She didn't even question me when I purchased a large bubble-padded envelope. Or when I took off my shoes and then removed my socks and placed them inside the envelope, sealing it shut. She seemed to be watching me helplessly as I slipped my shoes back on and then sauntered up to the counter. Using a post office pen, I wrote: *W. White, P.O. Box 8799, Toronto, ON, L8T 4S2* in the centre of the package. I left the return address blank.

I turned toward Hollis, holding the envelope up for her to see. I grinned. "You are as good as de-hexed."

"I know I'm going to regret asking," she said. "But why, Claire? Why are you sending the White Witch your stinky socks? And how in the world is that supposed to get me de-hexed?"

"Glad you asked," I said. "First, I'm sending my socks because I needed to send something and unless you're willing to give up those lovely dangling earrings …" Her hands shot to her ears in defence. "Yeah. I thought so. And how is this going to de-hex you, you ask? Easy-peasy, cheddar cheesy."

I placed the envelope on the counter and dinged the little silver bell once. A short, stocky clerk with mousy-brown hair appeared from the back room. She had a rather stern look about her.

"Hello," I said, politeness dripping from every sylla-ble. "I'd like to send this package special delivery. Same-day service."

The clerk took the envelope and placed it on a scale. Next, she got out a measuring tape and calculated its size. "That will be twenty-six dollars and thirty-five cents," she announced in a monotone voice.

I gulped. I knew my plan wasn't going to be cheap, but had had no clue as to just how expensive it was going to be. I dug into my pocket and pulled out a wad of crumpled bills and loose change. I calculated quickly. I had enough. Just enough. Enough to pay for the pack-age and get Hollis and me to the next and final stop in our journey. I didn't necessarily have enough money to get us home, but I made two split-second decisions:

1. I'd worry about that bridge when it was time to cross it (even if it meant having to go for a quick swim).
2. I would not disclose our financial crisis to Hollis.

This plan was going to work, I told myself. It was foolproof.

"Great," I said, handing over the money to the lady. I watched her place a computer-generated sticker on the envelope.

"No return address?" she asked. It sounded more like a statement given the lack of inflection in her voice. "It's always a good idea to include one in case the package gets lost."

I shook my head. "No worries. I'll be seeing this package again soon enough." She looked at me with a deadpan expression, shrugged her shoulders, and then placed the package on the counter behind her.

"So, um, when will it get sent out?" I asked.

"Shortly," she said. "I can guarantee it will get to its destination today."

"Perfect," I said. "That's all I need to know." I turned toward Hollis and ushered her a few steps away from the counter. "Now," I said, digging out Jordan's phone from my pocket. "All we need to do is find the post office box location …"

"Um, Claire," said Hollis.

"Not now," I said, connecting to the Internet and bringing up my favourite browser.

"But, Claire," said Hollis again, tugging on my sleeve.

I yanked it away. "Quit bugging me," I said. "Can't you see I'm trying to discover the location of the post office box?" I typed in *Reverse Postal Code Locator* and hit Enter.

"Claire, I think you should see this —" said Hollis.

"Honestly, Hollis. I've almost found the location of the post office box," I snarled. I quickly entered the postal code L8T 4S2 and pressed Enter again.

"Claire!" shouted Hollis, grabbing me by the shoulders and spinning me around to face the clerk at the counter. I looked up just in time to see her strolling out from behind the counter with my package under her arm! She held a set of keys. My jaw dropped as I watched her open a tiny metal door in the centre of a wall full of post office boxes.

I looked down at Jordan's phone. Post office boxes serving the postal code L8T 4S2 were in this very drug store!

Fuming, I jammed Jordan's cellphone into my pocket and marched, fists clenched, right up to the clerk just as she was locking the box.

"*This* is the location of the post office box?" I said, anger oozing from each and every pore. It was definitely meant to be a statement — a rather annoyed statement, I might add — but the clerk took it to be a question.

"I'm sorry," she responded dryly, "but I'm not at liberty to disclose that information."

"What? But I just saw you!" I said. "Do you mean to tell me that I just paid twenty-six dollars and thirty-five cents for you to walk five steps?"

"Five steps. Fifty kilometres. It's all the same to the post office, young lady," she said. Then, for the first time, she smiled. It was the kind of smile you just want to slap off someone's face. "I told you your package would arrive today."

21

"Now what?" asked Hollis, checking her watch. It was about a quarter to one.

"What do you mean, *now what?*" I said, rolling my eyes and shaking my head. To me it was as logical as lighting the fuse of a firecracker and then standing back and watching it explode. "We wait, of course."

"We wait." Hollis nodded.

"We wait." I nodded.

"And how long do we wait, Claire? Hours? Days? Months?" Her voice was rising again. I was afraid if it rose any higher, it might start shattering glass.

"Oh don't be ridiculous," I said. "The White Witch will come. She'll be here. She'll pick up her mail before the end of the day. I'm sure of it. I can feel it in my bones." I shivered for effect.

"Before the end of the day ..." Hollis echoed. She continued to nod. She was beginning to look like a little bobble-head. She also smiled sweetly — so sweetly I was lulled into a false sense of security. I almost didn't see it coming when she let loose and began attacking me. Her delicate hands flailed like a wild windmill. I had to grab hold of her wrists to stop the onslaught.

"Will you get control of yourself already?" I hissed. I

motioned my head toward the clerk who was eyeing us and frowning. "You're going to get us kicked out!"

She broke free from my grasp. After several deep breaths and some kind of yoga-Zen calming technique, Hollis had settled down enough for me to explain. I told her that I'd seen a doughnut shop across the street. We'd go and sit there. We'd watch every person who entered and exited the drug store. The one carrying our package would be the White Witch. I was pretty proud of myself for coming up with such a perfect plan under such incredible pressure. Hollis was skeptical as usual.

"I need to be home before my parents, or they will kill me. What if this White Witch person doesn't show? What if she picks up her mail after work?"

The thought had crossed my mind, but I'd quickly dismissed it. "No way. She's a writer. She probably works from home. She probably doesn't keep regular hours. She's coming. I don't know how I know. I just do. Listen, we still have a few hours before we need to be home. And I say *we*, Hollis, because *I* need to be home too, remember?"

Relief seeped into her expression. I think she figured if I needed to be home, too, she was safe.

"So we just hang out a while longer, okay?" I continued. "If we leave here empty-handed today, all we'll have lost is our time." I wriggled my uncomfortable toes. "And my socks."

I think she realized that at this point she had nothing left to lose. "You promise we'll leave no later than three o'clock?"

"Promise," I said. And I meant it. I really did. The only problem was bus fare. We technically still had enough money to get us home — if we didn't eat anything at the doughnut shop.

I crossed the street, hanging onto Hollis's arm while walking backwards. Probably not the safest thing to do, but I couldn't risk letting the drugstore out of my sight for even a nanosecond. I had to scrutinize every woman who entered and exited the place. With my rotten luck, I'd probably end up blinking and miss the White Witch altogether.

Inside the doughnut shop I snatched a seat by the window where there were several old stools along a thin counter. Hollis insisted on having a pop and a cruller. I dug into my pocket and tried not to let her see I was counting. There wasn't enough money, and though visions of apple fritters danced in my head, I fought the urge to scarf one down.

"Here you go," I said, handing her a couple of bucks. "Knock yourself out."

"Don't you want anything?" she asked.

"Nah," I lied. "I'm not hungry. That stromboli was really filling." I patted my stomach.

For the longest time I sat gazing at the drugstore entrance. A few women came and went, but none that looked even remotely like a White Witch. I got excited at one point when this woman with long, blond hair wearing a red poncho walked in. I sprang from my seat and was poised to bolt out the door, but the woman exited the store empty-handed. I sunk back down onto my stool. I leaned on the counter, holding my head in my hands, trying to focus my mind on the White Witch. Maybe I could somehow channel her with my thoughts and drag her to her mailbox telepathically. Okay. I was getting desperate.

Hollis was sipping her pop and nibbling on her cruller. All the while, I contemplated exactly what a White Witch might look like. Was she tall and thin or short and stocky? Maybe she was tall and stocky. Did she have brown hair? Black hair? Chestnut hair with auburn highlights? For some reason, I kept thinking blond. No — not blond — silver-white. And old. Yes, she was very old. Maybe hundreds of years old. She would most likely be wearing Gothic-style clothing. Definitely something draping. A cape, of course. That was it. I had a clear vision of the person I was seeking and my posture swelled with new confidence.

Maybe it was this new confidence, or maybe it was that after a half hour of staring out the window I was slightly bored. Whatever the reason, I suddenly found myself blurting out, "So why exactly do you hate me, Hollis?"

"What?" she said, practically choking on her last bite of cruller.

"You heard me," I said, keeping my eyes trained on the drugstore. "I know you do. I just want to know why."

"I-I don't *hate* you," she stammered.

"You're such liar," I said, cutting her off. I could feel my cheeks getting warm, but I refused to look at her. I wasn't going to miss the White Witch, not even for the chance to watch Hollis squirm. "You have been on my case forever. You are always making fun of me. Don't you think I know what you and your gargoyle friends are all saying about me?"

I think when you have enough nerve to ask a direct question, you end up giving people the courage to give you a direct answer, because that's exactly what happened.

"Look, Claire. It's pretty hard not to laugh at you. You're always doing these really goofy things."

"Oh, so I'm *goofy*, am I?" Deep in my gut, I knew there was some truth to what she was saying — knowing is one thing, but hearing someone actually say it out loud is another.

"Yes. Goofy," she said. "Like that time you came to school speaking with a German accent."

"You made me feel like a total idiot!" I said.

"Trust me, you didn't need my help. You were doing fine all on your own."

I glared out the window. A little old lady with silver-white hair had just entered the drugstore. I barely took notice of her. How dare Hollis call me an idiot? Foreign accents were cool. What did she know?

"It wasn't German. It was actually Scandinavian, if you must know," I spat.

"*Vot vos zat?*" she said, breaking into hysterical laughter. I wanted to slug her. It took every last bit of energy in my body to restrain myself and keep watching the drugstore. A really tall, bald man entered. He was wearing a Miami Dolphins football jersey over a turtleneck sweater. He was so huge that he might have actually been a football player or basketball player — almost seven feet tall. He had to duck to pass through the doorframe.

"And what about that time you came to school wearing two different shoes?" she said. "Oh — and how about the time your eyebrows disappeared?"

Now Hollis was just plain asking for it. My fingers curled into a fist — my skin stretching white over my knuckles. But before I could raise my hand, she spoke.

"Anyway," she said, her laughter dying and her expression morphing into something serious, "I guess that's what I hate about you …"

My fingers slackened and my brow furled. Three more people entered the drugstore, but I couldn't begin to tell you what they looked like, I was so taken aback by Hollis's comment. I forgot what I was supposed to be doing and turned to face her.

"… the fact that you not only were *allowed* to come to school looking like that, but the fact that you actually *did*."

Something had changed — but I wasn't quite getting it yet. Why in the world would Hollis hate me for going to school eyebrowless or wearing two different shoes? Laugh at me? Sure. Tease me? Okay. But hate me? I didn't get it.

"First off," she continued, "my mother examines me tip to toe and has to approve every single strand of hair before she lets me out of the house. Wearing two different shoes? Ha!" Hollis scoffed. "She'd sooner lock me in a closet for the rest of my life than to let me out of the house looking like that."

I was beginning to understand. Hollis's mother was a control freak. She forced her to enter those beauty pageants. She made her dress so perfectly. Act perfectly. It wasn't so much that Hollis never did anything wrong — it was that she wasn't *allowed* to do anything wrong!

"And maybe even worse," Hollis said, her voice dropping to a whisper, "is that, even if by some bizarre fluke my mother actually let me go looking like that, I just couldn't. I'd die a thousand deaths. The other girls would never let me live it down. They watch me like a hawk, just waiting for me to mess up so that they can pounce on me."

For a second, Hollis looked almost sad — helpless — then her expression changed again. "... and there *you* are," she said, her voice now thick with resentment, "walking around without a care in the world. You do whatever you want without a thought as to what others think or say."

And there it was. Hollis didn't hate me — she resented me. She was not this stuck-up snob all full of herself. She was insecure. Deathly afraid to fall off her high pedestal.

"I don't get it," I said. "Why would Tiffany and Tenisha want you to mess up? They're your friends."

"Friends?" She gave a wry chuckle. "Is that what you call them?"

Hollis had lost me again. Why wouldn't they be her friends? They were always around her giggling and gossiping. They did everything together at school. Isn't that what you call friendship? Paula-Jean and I hung around because she was my BFF. Even when she was madder than spit at me, deep down I knew Paula-Jean was still my best friend.

"You're so naive, Claire," said Hollis. "Tiffany, Tenisha, Cheyenne — they only hang around me because I'm popular. It makes them popular, too. They suck up to me like there's no tomorrow. But they don't mean any of it. And I know it. They'd love to see me go down. And like a bunch of vultures they'd be all over me picking my bones clean."

The image was vile. But I kind of liked thinking of those girls as vultures — a bit of a change from gargoyles.

"So why do you hang around them?" I said.

She rubbed her temples with her fingertips. Headache, I thought. A big one.

"Who else do I have?" she asked.

My silence spoke volumes.

"Exactly," she said. "You say, *I* hate you, Claire — but you're the one who hates me."

I was fighting myself. I didn't want to admit she was right. Maybe it wasn't just that she hated me — maybe I was part and parcel to all the hating. And maybe it was time I admitted a few things to Hollis and to myself.

"Okay. Maybe there's a crumb of truth in what you're saying. Hate is a strong word. Maybe I, well, *dislike* you. A little," I said. "But it's because you're so perfect. And you're so pretty. And popular. And I'm …well, I'm … I guess I'm just not."

"Look, Claire," said Hollis, "sometimes, you've just got to make peace with reality."

I frowned. "What's that supposed to mean?"

"Well, accept the fact that you're not the most beautiful girl in the world, for starters."

My jaw felt limp. I heard her, but I couldn't believe what she was saying. She was horrible. Awful. The meanest person I'd ever met. "Easy for you to say, since you are."

"Me? Are you kidding?" She laughed. "If all those beauty pageants have taught me anything, it's that there is always, and I mean *always*, someone prettier out there. It's like I said, you just need to make peace with reality."

I looked at Hollis. And then I knew. She wasn't so different from me, after all. In fact, I think we were a lot alike.

I opened my mouth to say something. Then I closed it. This time, I was actually going to think before I spoke. Should I apologize to her for all the nasty things I'd ever thought and said about her? Should I tell her I finally understood her? Should I tell her I was happy I'd cursed her — since it gave us a chance to get to know each other? I decided to just reach over and give her a great big Claire-bear hug.

I flung my arms around her. At first, I could feel her body bristle, but then she let loose and hugged me back. It was a great moment and it may have actually led to some sort of lasting friendship-type-thing, if I hadn't looked over her shoulder and out the window. At that very moment, I saw something that turned my entire world upside down — someone was leaving the drugstore carrying my big bubble envelope.

22

I shoved Hollis aside, nearly knocking her off her stool. It killed our touching moment.

"Hey!" she shouted, but there was no time to explain. I was already halfway out the door.

I danced side to side, waiting for a lull in the traffic. By the time it was safe to cross, Hollis was hanging on to me and I was dragging her across the street, chasing after my runaway bubble-package.

"Wait!" I shouted. "Stop!" But my package kept moving, weaving in and out of pedestrian-traffic like a running-back heading for a touchdown.

I let go of Hollis, who couldn't keep up, and broke into a full-blown sprint. I nearly knocked several people over, including the old lady I'd seen enter the drugstore, before I caught up to my package. Reaching out, I grabbed hold of the shiny teal and orange shirt of its captor. I dug my heels into the concrete, and managed to bring the guy to a standstill. He swung round to face me — all seven feet of him — swatting at my hand like I was some kind of insect.

"You stole it!" I shouted up at him. "You stole my package!"

"What?" said the guy in the Miami Dolphins jersey. "What are you going on about, little lady?"

I was fuming. This guy had completely, totally, and miserably blown my most awesome plan. I didn't know how he did it, but he had stolen my package and ruined everything and I wasn't about to let him get away with it.

"My package!" I said, anger shooting like sparks from every fibre of my being. I pointed an accusing finger at the bubble-envelope. "How did you get hold of *my* package!"

I could tell by his expression that he was more than confused than angry. "*Your* package?" he said. He held out the envelope for me to see. "Now that's funny. How did *your* package go and get itself addressed to *me* and get placed in *my* mail box?"

Wham! I felt like I'd just been run over by the entire Miami defensive line. Impossible. No way. Not a chance. I shook my head. The world around me began to spin. I suddenly felt sick to my stomach. I thought I was going to heave all over the guy's giant white Nikes. I closed my eyes and took several deep breaths. When my stomach settled, I opened my eyes. I reached into my pocket and pulled out my little green book. I held it in my trembling hands, running my fingers across the author's name. The White Witch. Hollis had caught up with us by now. She volleyed glances between me, the book, and the enormous man standing in front of me.

"It can't be," I said, my voice quivering. "You're not a … a … a …"

"A *witch?*" he said, eyeing the book and smiling warmly.

"You're not even … wha … wha—"

"*White?*" he said, his grin spreading like butter across his lips.

How could this be? I wracked my brain. How could I have been this wrong about something I was so absolutely sure of?

"*You* are W. White?" I said, disbelief echoing in every syllable.

"Sure am," he said. "Wayne White. At your service." He tipped his head. Then he took the book from my hands, flipping through the pages. His eyes were twinkling like he was remembering an old friend. "I see you've read one of my books." He held it out for me.

I took a step back. No way. This was all wrong. This couldn't be happening. W. White was a witch. A woman. A White Witch who was going to help me de-hex Hollis.

I felt myself deflating like a punctured beachball. Poor Hollis. What was I going to do now? I'd cursed her and then promised her I'd fix everything. I dragged her out of her home and through the city. And for what? For it all to end like this? I looked at her apologetically. She didn't say a word. I could tell she was thinking the same thing. She took the book from the man and gently placed it into my hands.

Tears welled in my eyes. "I-I used your b-book to cast a binding spell on my friend. And I lost the string and I can't remove the spell. I-I was hoping the White Witch — I mean, *you* could wave your magic wand or something and fix everything."

He stared at me for what felt like an eternity. He was still smiling, but something in his eyes had changed — I felt those two dark pools looking right into me. Right through me.

"I'm afraid I can't help you," he said quietly. "I have no magic powers."

My heart felt like it had fallen into quicksand and was sinking fast. This guy was my last hope. He just had to be able to help me. "But, you wrote this book," I said. "You *are* the White Witch, even if you don't look like one. Can't you do something? Anything?"

He sighed and shook his head. "I wrote that book all right. But I'm not the person you're looking for. I'm a writer. I write things. I wrote a bunch of those little books, you know, *Cheeses and Chutneys*, *The Best of Bananas*. It pays the bills — tides me over until I can publish what I'm really passionate about."

"And what's that?" asked Hollis.

"Poetry," he said.

This was great. Just great. I went on a wild and crazy journey to find a little white witch and what I found was a seven-foot poet. Still, I'd come this close and I wasn't going to give up that easily. "So you're telling me this book isn't magic?" I said. "You're saying it has no magic power whatsoever? That I didn't really cast any spells?"

He took a deep breath and put a hand on my shoulder. He slowly shook his head.

Hollis began to sniffle. I think the reality of her situation was sinking in. If the book had no power and I didn't actually hex her — then she was really and truly sick. And what was worse, there was nothing I, or any witch, could do to help her.

I just wouldn't accept it. I couldn't. "But my zit ...

and Jordan ... and Hollis ..." I said, my voice fading to a whisper. "I was so sure ..."

"Not everything in life is what it appears to be," he said, taking his hand from my shoulder. "Nothing is simple, either. Life isn't ever black or white. Mostly it's just shades of grey."

For a second, Wayne White reminded me a lot of my father. That made me think of my parents — of Hollis's parents. I needed to get Hollis home. I'd caused her enough trouble, might as well get her home on time, if nothing else.

"I-I'm sorry. I didn't mean to bother you," I said to Wayne White. I turned toward Hollis and took her gently by the arm. "Come on. Let's go home."

Slowly, we started walking toward the streetcar stop. Over my shoulder, I heard Wayne White say, "My grandma used to say believin' goes a long way ..."

Perfect. Exactly what I needed. I came all this way and dragged Hollis along just for some stupid saying my father could have tossed at me back home. Home. It suddenly felt a long way away. And it was going to get even longer still.

"Now remember," I said to Hollis, as the streetcar approached. "Take the northbound subway to Finch Station. From there, take the 2A bus. It will bring you right to your street."

Her face contorted. "What? Why are you giving me directions? You're coming, aren't you?"

I could see panic flash in her eyes as I shook my head. She began to argue as the streetcar buzzed to a halt and the doors smacked open. I grabbed her hand and placed the bus fare in her palm — the last of my money. "Remember, the 2A."

I ushered her on board. I could still hear her cursing long after the doors sealed shut. I stood there watching the streetcar disappear down Queen Street. I suddenly felt very alone.

I reached into my pocket and pulled out Jordan's phone. Just before I began to dial, I noticed a white spot on my shoulder where Wayne had put his hand. Could it possibly be clown makeup?

23

"Hey," I said, after Mac passed the phone to Jordan. "Hey," said Jordan. "Where are you?"

"Um, downtown," I muttered.

After a pause that felt like hours he asked, "You okay? You don't sound so good."

Standing alone at the corner of Queen and Dovercourt, I was fighting a losing battle with my emotions. Jordan's question gave my feelings a huge advantage. I couldn't contain them any longer. I started blubbering uncontrollably.

"I'm stuck. I have no money to get home. I don't know what to do. Can you come get me, Jordan? I'll be nice to you from now on. I won't bug you. And I'll never thrash you again — not even indirectly — I swear!"

"Indirectly thrash whaa?" he said. I was too far gone now to respond in any sort of coherent manner. The rest of what came out of me was a jumble of syllables, sounds, and sniffles mingled with some quite alien-sounding utterances.

"Whoa! Claire!" he shouted. I heard him say something muffled by his hand on the receiver. I swallowed great gulps of air trying to calm myself. "Hang on," he said. "I'm coming."

He stayed on the phone long enough to find out my exact location. I told him about the doughnut shop where Hollis and I had stalked the not-so-white not-so-witch. He told me to wait inside. To tell the employees, if they tried to kick me out, that I was just waiting for him and he'd buy some coffee and some doughnuts when he arrived. I collected what was left of my nerve and did as he said.

It was a long hour while I waited for Jordan to arrive. At least the doughnut shop employees seemed to take pity on me and didn't get on my case for loitering. As I sat in the exact same spot I'd been sitting not long ago with Hollis, I wondered how she was faring. I wondered if she'd gotten home in time or if I'd gotten her in trouble with her parents. I was worried about her — I really was. And not just about her journey home, but about her health. If I hadn't truly hexed her I wondered what could be causing all her issues. The numbness in her left hand. Her left foot dragging. The headaches. No matter which way I looked at it, it wasn't good. I was so angry at myself for ever wishing her harm. I felt lower than dirt for delighting in her misfortune. I came to the conclusion that I definitely had some serious character cleansing to undergo.

As soon as I saw Jordan through the window I sprang from my seat and raced to the door. I threw myself at him, giving him the biggest hug I can remember. And the weirdest thing was that he let me. He actually let me. I mean, it wasn't as if he hugged me back or anything, but he let me hug him and that was enough. I had so many things I wanted to say, but didn't know where to begin. He helped me out by simply saying, "Come on, Claire. Let's go home."

I was shocked when Jordan led me around the corner from the doughnut shop to where my father sat in his car waiting. I flashed Jordan an angry look, but it quickly melted to gratitude once I was sitting safely inside the car.

"We'll talk about this later with your mother," said my dad, after reaching back and giving me a huge kiss on the cheek. "You might as well take in all the daylight you can, Claire-bear — since other than going to school, you won't be seeing much of it for a very long time."

Grounded. Figures. And yet somehow the idea of sitting safely at home, tucked away in my room, wasn't remotely unappealing.

"Does Mom know?" I asked, hesitantly. Mom was the heavy hand. A good, solid six months of grounding was getting off easy with her.

"Sure does," said my father. "She wanted to be here as well ... but ..." His voice suddenly changed. I could feel he was choking back something. After a long pause during which I could tell he was reining in his emotions, he continued, "But she's with Cyrus right now at the vet's. I wasn't going to tell you until we got home, but Cyrus wasn't doing so well today. He was throwing up a lot and refusing to eat and Mom had to take him to see the vet."

"Cyrus!" I said, my voice sounding more like a yelp. I looked at Jordan and then at my father's eyes in the rear-view mirror. They were looking at each other, as if sharing a secret. "What's wrong with him? Tell me he's okay!"

Yet another piece of my world came crashing down on top of me. I'd been so mean to my dog lately, my sweet, grouchy, little beagle. I'd treated him as rotten as everyone else in my life. A wave of nausea rolled through my body.

"Take it easy, honey," said my father. "He's going to be okay. He had to have an emergency operation. Apparently the poor guy had some kind of knotted piece of string stuck inside his intestines."

At that point I think I must have passed out, because all I remember is the world outside my window fading to black.

24

I held Cyrus in my trembling hands. I didn't even try to fight back my tears. He was weak and was wearing one of those cone-like contraptions to keep him from picking at his bandage. He still managed to lift his pointy little snout and stare at me, his amber eyes sad and helpless.

"I'm sorry," I whispered into his velvety ear. "I am so sorry."

He tried to growl in typical Cyrus-style, but not much sound came out.

"I know," I said. "You were right. You were right about everything." Satisfied that he'd finally won the argument, Cyrus laid his head in my lap and closed his eyes to rest.

I sat cradling him in my lap for over an hour. I had been so horribly mean to him and I was completely responsible for his terrible condition. Never for a second did I think he'd go and eat the darn knotted string.

My mother actually brought the disgusting thing home in a little plastic baggie. It was the most vile thing I'd ever seen, all covered in wet mucus-y gunk. But it was definitely recognizable. It was mine all right. No mistaking it.

"Do you know anything about this, Claire?" asked my mother, holding the baggie up for me to see.

With downcast eyes, puffy and red from crying, I told my parents the whole story. They were really good about it, I have to say, since they actually let me tell the entire story without interrupting me even once. I think they thought I'd lost my mind because when I was done, my mother shook her head.

"Claire," she said. "Even if you could do magic, you can't go around trying to hex everyone who you don't get along with."

"I know that now, Mom," I said. "Believe me, I've learned my lesson. And I know this is going to sound really nuts, but I wish I had hexed Hollis. I mean, at least then I'd be able to de-hex her. She's really sick, you know."

I'd tried calling Hollis several times since I got home, but there was no answer at her house. I couldn't shake the horrible feeling that was growing in the pit of my stomach. I don't know how I knew it, but I knew something was really wrong.

My father, who had sat silently throughout my bizarre explanation, finally spoke. I braced myself as he opened his mouth. I was ready for it. I knew what was coming. At least I thought I did.

"I'm glad you've learned your lesson, Claire. I'm also glad you're taking responsibility for your actions. I hope you realize now that when people don't get along it's never one hundred percent one person's fault." He put his arm around me. "Hollis is going to be just fine," he said. "You have to believe it. Sometimes believing goes a long way."

Wham! I couldn't believe it. His words hit me square in the jaw. Those were the exact words the White Witch — I mean, Wayne White — had told me! This was weird. Really weird. He and my father both wanted me to believe. But how was my believing going to help Hollis? I hadn't quite figured that out yet.

Though I was technically grounded, my parents let me continue to call Hollis until it was really late. There was no way I was going to sleep until I knew she was okay. It was almost ten o'clock, when Hollis's father finally answered the phone. What he told me made my blood run cold. I listened, barely hearing his words. I felt paper-thin, like everything that had happened — everything that was happening — was happening in some sort of parallel two-dimension reality.

Cyrus wasn't the only one who had to have emergency surgery. According to her father, when Hollis got home from her city trek with me, her headache was excruciating. Her parents found her writhing in pain. They rushed her to the Hospital for Sick Kids, where she had to have an emergency MRI. It was the last test she was scheduled for the next day. The doctors discovered she had a lump in the lining of her brain and had to remove it immediately.

His words ran me over like a freight train. I couldn't breathe. It was like there wasn't enough oxygen in the whole world to fill even half my lungs. I gasped, struggling for air, but ended up coughing and choking on it.

I had to say something. I had to force my lips to move. Force the words out of my mouth. The sound was scratchy and high-pitched — a voice that wasn't my own.

"I-is sh-she going to b-be ok-kay?"

"Time will tell," said her father. "Tonight is critical. I just came home to get Hollis's mother a few things and then I'm heading back to the hospital."

For the first time in my life I was at a complete loss for words. Things that usually came shooting out of my mouth like lightning were blocked behind the boulder-sized lump in my throat. I tried to swallow, but I couldn't manage enough spit.

"She knew you would call," said Mr. Van Horn suddenly.

My stomach did back flips as my mind struggled to keep up with what he was saying.

"Hollis knew you would call, Claire," repeated her father. "She kept muttering, '*Tell Claire it's okay. Tell Claire it's not her fault.*' I don't know what she meant, but I'm guessing you do."

For the second time that day, tears spilled down my cheeks. I don't know how I managed to get the words out, but I asked if I could visit her. Her father said he'd let me know in the morning. Before he hung up, I said, "Tell Hollis ... tell Hollis ..." but I couldn't finish my sentence.

"I'll tell her," he said. And then he hung up.

I hadn't even noticed, but my parents and Jordan had gathered round me while I was on the phone. Between gulping sobs, I managed to tell them about

Hollis's surgery. Jordan was the first to reach over and give me a hug.

It was almost midnight when I finally went up to bed. I laid my head on my pillow and tried to sleep, but it wouldn't come. There was something that was bothering me. Something niggling at the back of my brain, struggling to break free. It was like a word you can't come up with, a word you know perfectly well, yet it's hiding in the shadows of your mind.

When the clock in the hall began to strike midnight, it was like the fog in my brain suddenly cleared and I knew exactly what I had to do.

Sometimes, believing goes a long way …

"Of course!" I said, sitting bolt-upright in my bed. I thumped the side of my mattress. "Why didn't I think of it sooner?"

I scrambled out of my bed and raced down the stairs. I opened the door to the garage and rummaged through the trash for the little baggie containing the disgusting shoelace. Locating it, I raced back to my bedroom with the plastic bag in my hands and searched the floor for my jeans. I dug out my little green book and then turned on my bedside lamp. I flipped frantically though the pages until I found the Binding Hex. Wrinkling my nose and holding my breath, I opened the baggie and took out the nasty shoelace. I shuddered as I held the gross thing in my hands. But nothing was going to stop me from what I now knew I needed to do. I took a deep breath, and, digging my fingernails into each of the seven knots, I began to untie them, one by one, all the while chanting:

Un-shut the mouth,
Un-seal the eyes,
Un-clasp the limbs,
Un-tie the ties
Un-block the ears,
Un-twist the toe,
Un-hold the heart,
Un-bind my foe.
No longer hast thou caused me harm,
By notion, word, or deed,
Now thought, word, and deed with kindness has
    been done,
Now you and I are free.

25

My mother found me in the morning, lying in a curled-up ball on the floor in my bedroom, still clutching the untied shoelace. Though I searched high and low, there was no sign of my little green book. The funny thing was, though I had had very little sleep, I felt like a new person. I felt like my limbs and my tongue were back to normal. No more tingling tongue. No more wooden feet.

Like he'd promised, Hollis's father called in the morning. He said that Hollis was doing surprisingly well. That the lump had been a small tumour. Luckily it was benign and what's more, it had been in the best possible spot so as not to cause any permanent brain damage. He said that Hollis would have to take it slow for a long time, but she would definitely make a full recovery. And what's more, she'd said she really wanted to see me.

My parents allowed me to take the morning off school. I was so excited I couldn't see straight. And though I tripped running up the stairs to get ready — it felt different somehow. Like it was just clumsy old me again.

My father took the morning off work and drove me to the hospital. I couldn't wait to see Hollis. Of course I believed her father that she was going to be okay, but I

needed to see for myself. The drive into the city took forever. When we finally got there, we parked in the under-
ground lot and took the elevator up. I insisted on buying
Hollis some flowers and a stuffed animal in the gift shop.
As I walked through the sterile halls, I couldn't help but
keep an eye out for a very tall, very peculiar clown.

Hollis was in a private room. As I approached, I figured the man standing outside her room must be her
father. We introduced ourselves. He shook hands with my
father, then reached over and gave me a hug. He motioned
for me to enter. I could hear several voices inside the
room. I took a deep breath and walked up to the open
door. I knocked just to let her know I was coming in.

When I saw her, I felt the tears begin to well in my
eyes. She was lying in bed, wearing one of those hideous
green hospital gowns. On her head, she wore a kerchief.
Her long blond hair cascaded out the back of the kerchief on one side, but the other side was sparse. I realized she'd had to have her head partially shaved for the
operation. Her mother sat in a chair on one side of the
bed, holding Hollis's hand. On the other side, Tiffany
and Tenisha were squished into the other large chair.

When Hollis saw me, her sea-foam eyes lit up and
she smiled. Everyone else stopped talking and stared at
me. I suddenly felt really out of place. Then Hollis said,
"I'm so glad you came."

Slowly, I walked toward her and placed the flowers
and stuffed animal at the foot of her bed.

"Thanks," she said. Then she turned toward the others, "Could you guys give Claire and me a few minutes?"

Tiffany's brow wrinkled. Tenisha mumbled a quick, "Uh, sure." They both left the room in awkward silence. Hollis's mother didn't move a muscle. She sat smiling at Hollis holding her hand.

"You too, Mom," said Hollis.

Her mother bristled. She gave me a strange look, but then stood up. "Of course, Hollis. Whatever you want, dear."

Once she'd left the room, Hollis asked me to sit down. I sank into the same chair Tenisha and Tiffany had occupied. I was fighting back the tears. It killed me seeing her like this. It had been so easy to hate her in her designer clothes and her movie-star hair.

After a long pause, she spoke.

"The doctor said the tumour was probably there for a long time and only recently began to grow. The pressure caused my headaches and the numbness in my left hand and foot."

All I could do was sit and nod and listen.

"She said I was pretty lucky because the tumour wasn't actually in my brain but in the lining of my brain. She said I'm going to be okay."

I nodded again, acutely aware of the tears threatening to spill down my cheeks.

"I just want you to know you didn't do this to me. And our little adventure in the city didn't cause it, either." She smiled and I knew she meant it. Then she added, "I've been mean to you in the past, Claire, and I'm sorry for it. I'm sorry I resented you and I'm sorry I talked about you behind your back." Then she reached over and took my hand. "And you know what? I actually had fun yesterday with you. It was the craziest thing I'd ever done in my life — okay, totally bizarre — but it was fun. And ..." she continued cautiously, "I think I do believe in magic now, Claire. I really do. Only, I think being alive — that's the real magic."

I squeezed her hand back. I was thinking so many thoughts they all tangled up in my mind and left me speechless. I knew a response was in order, but I couldn't seem to make my mouth form words. I'd made a mental decision not to tell her I still thought I was responsible for her condition. She was happy. And she was okay. That was all that mattered. Still, I had to say something. I cleared my throat.

"You look awful," I said.

We both burst out laughing.

I left the hospital feeling a whole lot lighter, like I could float up to the sky. As my father and I got into the elevator taking us down to the parking garage I turned to him and hugged him spontaneously. I was about to let go just as the elevator doors were closing, when I swear I caught a glimpse of orange polka dot pants and puffy sleeves and huge Nike shoes disappearing around the corner.

26

My grounding lasted for two weeks. I spent the entire time searching my room for my little green book. It had vanished.

Though I wasn't allowed to have anyone over during that time, Paula-Jean and I managed to get caught up during recesses. No one else would have believed a word I said, but Paula-Jean did. She was the best friend anyone could have and I made a point of telling her each and every day just how much her friendship meant to me.

By the end of my grounding, Hollis was home from the hospital. Though, it would be another week or two before she was allowed to go to school. She called me once and we had a really nice chat. She said she never did see any clown at the hospital and though she asked several nurses, no one could either confirm or deny any such person helping out in the huge hospital.

Now that everything was slowly getting back to normal, I realized I had one last thing I had to do.

My first day of being un-grounded, I called Paula-Jean and asked if she would come by my house after school. Paula-Jean being Paula-Jean, agreed to help me with my plan.

I bought the holly bush at the nursery with money I'd borrowed from Jordan. Since they were fresh out of dwarf winterberry euonymuses, I was hoping that Mrs. Walker would like the holly bush just as much. At least it was a winter blooming bush. I made up my mind to visit Mrs. Walker once a week and help with her gardening come the spring. In the meantime, I'd told her I'd shovel her snow throughout the winter. Like the clown said, *you can always find a way to help out in your community if you really want to.* Mrs. Walker accepted my apology, my holly bush, and my offer of help. She seemed genuinely excited about someone coming over to chat with her about her shrubbery.

Satisfied I'd set everything right, I headed home. Paula-Jean and I parted at the corner. I thanked her for helping me fix things with Mrs. Walker. She gave me a hug and then headed for her house. I watched her disappear around the corner. I swore to myself I'd never take our friendship for granted again.

As for Hollis, I wouldn't say we became good friends or anything, but let's just say we began to tolerate each other's presence a whole lot better. You could say we *made peace with reality.* And, as unbelievable as it sounds, Hollis actually signed up to read to little kids at the hospital on weekends as soon as she was well enough to do so. She convinced her mother she wanted to do it in place of modelling classes. And even more unbelievable, her mother agreed. Apparently Hollis thought she needed some character-cleansing after all.

As I made my way home I began to wonder about

Wayne White. Who and what was he really? A writer? A publisher? A clown? A — dare I think it — witch?

I suppose in some way I got my answer. As I approached my house I saw something sitting on my doorstep. It was a plain, somewhat ragged bubble envelope. The name W. White and the post office box were crossed out and above it I saw my name scrawled across the top. No address. No postal code. Nothing but my name. I reached down and picked up the familiar envelope. I ripped it open, reached in and pulled out the contents. My socks. My sweaty, stinky socks.

In all the confusion in the city, I'd forgotten to ask Wayne White to give them back to me. Apparently, he had returned them after all. The thing was, I never gave him my address. As a matter of fact, I had never even told him my name.

I was about to head inside when something else fell out of the envelope. Of all things, it was my little green book! I held it for a moment in my hands, wondering. Then, for some reason, I opened it to the very first page. There was something I hadn't noticed before. A foreword.

> There is a great power that dwells in each
> of us — a power to alter oneself, others,
> and the world around. Seek to control the
> energy deep within your spirit, live wisely,
> and, above all, do no harm — then, and
> only then will peace and harmony be yours.
> The White Witch

I smiled. Closing the book, I opened the door and headed into my house. Cyrus was waiting for me. I reached down and gave him a scratch behind the ear. He looked at me, then looked at the book in my other hand and snorfled.

"I know, Cyrus," I said, smiling. "I know."

Also by Marina Cohen

MIND GAP
978-1554888016
$9.99

Fourteen-year-old Jake MacRae's life is spinning out of control. He's making all the wrong choices — gambling, drinking, hanging around gang members — and now he's been asked to make a "special delivery." What should he do? Before he has a chance to make up his mind, Jake receives a mysterious text message inviting him to a flash party on a midnight subway train. As he steps off the platform and onto the ghostly 1950s-style Gloucester car, he has no idea he has just boarded a train bound for his worst nightmare. And what's more — he can't get off!

GHOST RIDE
978-1554884384
$12.99

Finalist for the Red Maple Award!

Sam McLean is less than thrilled with the prospect of moving to Ringwood. A nobody at his old school, fourteen-year-old Sam is desperate to be accepted by the cool kids and latches on to Cody Barns, aka Maniac. Cody's claim to fame is performing wild stunts — the crazier the better — and posting them on his blog. When Sam reluctantly joins Cody and his sidekick, Javon, on their midnight ghost riding, a practice in which the driver and passenger climb onto the hood of their moving car and dance, something goes terribly wrong. Cody convinces Sam to flee the scene, leaving Javon for dead. But soon mysterious messages appear on Cody's blog and anonymous notes are slid into Sam's locker. As Sam struggles with his conscience, a haunting question remains: Who else knows the truth?

Available at your favourite bookseller.

DUNDURN
www.dundurn.com

What did you think of this book?
Visit www.dundurn.com for reviews,
videos, updates, and more!